D0916910

TUR LARGE PRINT
Turnbull, Agnes Sligh, 1888-

Many a green isle

OCT 3 1 1985

DATE DUE			
MAR. 5 1987			
APR. 1 4 1987			
JAN 2 9 1988			
APR 22 '91			
APR. 2 9 1994			
NOV 5 1994			
NOV 2 2 1994			
JUN. 0 1 1995			
JUN. 1 5 1995			
OCT. 3 2 1995			
JUN 1 7 1992			

CONN. STATE LIBRARY
LIBRARY SERVICE CENTER
WILLIMANTIC, CONN.

OCT 3 1 1985

Also available in Large Print
by Agnes Sligh Turnbull:

The Golden Journey
Gown of Glory
The King's Orchard
The Nightingale
The Two Bishops
The Wedding Bargain
The Winds of Love

Agnes Sligh Turnbull

Many a Green Isle

CONNECTICUT STATE LIBRARY
LIBRARY DEVELOPMENT DIVISION
LIBRARY SERVICE CENTER
WILLIMANTIC, CONNECTICUT

G.K.HALL &CO.
Boston, Massachusetts
1985

TUR
LARGE
PRINT

Copyright © 1968 by Agnes Sligh Turnbull.

All rights reserved.

Published in Large Print by arrangement with
Houghton Mifflin Co.

British Commonwealth rights courtesy of
John Farquharson Ltd.

G.K. Hall Large Print Book Series.

Set in 18 pt English Times

Library of Congress Cataloging in Publication Data

Turnbull, Agnes Sligh, 1888-
  Many a green isle.

  (G.K. Hall Large print book series)
  1. Large type books. I. Title.
[PS3539.U76M3 1985]   813'.52   85-846
ISBN 0-8161-3645-9 (lg. print)

Many a green isle needs must be
In the deep wide sea of Misery . . .

From ''Lines Written Among
the Euganean Hills''
by Percy Bysshe
Shelley

One

THERE IS A certain type of American county seat town which just escapes being an overgrown village by the presence of a usually ornate stone courthouse in its midst. One comes upon these small cities which have been mysteriously dignified by the law in every state of the Union, more frequently perhaps in the east, but not now along the great highways. They cling, rather, to the older arteries which used to confound motorists as they studied their maps and then made their slow and often profane progress through the traffic of the narrow main streets. These, oddly enough, seem always to be fringed by the same shops and stores in every such town as though some unimaginative planner had devised them all.

Such a county seat was Marsden. It had, however, a double claim to importance for there was an institution of learning on the edge of town, known colloquially simply as *The College,* which was much older than the present seat of the law itself.

On a late April afternoon, the time being nearly five o'clock, the westering sun was sending a few bright slanting shafts across the golden dome of the courthouse (built, as it had been said bitterly by men at the time, by graft and gilded by corruption) and gave a last lightening to the dingy stores and office buildings that lined the central area of Main Street. Of course Lane's Department Store held a certain *tone* which communicated itself somewhat to the lesser mercantile sisters in its shadow: Ladies' Fancy Footwear, Delia's Lingerie, and the La Rose Dress Shop; but there was a casual shabbiness born of long acceptance to the outer aspects of Davis Drugs, Wells's Bakery, the Five and Ten, and the Community Shoe Store, just as the three-story office buildings of weathered brick which housed innumerable lawyers, a few doctors, along with Real Estate agents and salesmen, bore the marks of an almost unnoted age.

Along the street now walked briskly a strong looking man in his forties, with keen gray eyes, a firm chin with a Scotch dimple in it and a pleasant, rather quizzical expression as though mankind with all its frailties presented an interesting and on the whole rather attractive problem to him.

He swung along with his briefcase, speaking often to those who hailed him as he passed.

"Hi, Professor! How are you?"

"Fine, fine. Lovely weather, this!"

He passed the central business and professional section, and slowed up a little as the pavement began to rise under his feet. At the end of this small hill on another slightly larger on the edge of town stood the house that had been home to his family now for nearly ten years. Before he reached the end of this particular thoroughfare, however, there was an old yellow brick edifice where he often stopped. The occupant was Judge McWhorter, retired, and he could now be descried sitting on his small front porch behind its wrought iron railing.

"Well, Gavin," he said as the younger man came up, "you're late. Was the young idea not shootin' properly today? Come on up an' set a spell. I'm lonesome."

While over the years the wisdom of the Judge's decisions, couched in meticulous and at times even eloquent English, had been quoted and copied all over the state and beyond, his language now in speaking partook richly of the colloquial.

"I'd better explain something," he had told Gavin soon after they had first met. "There is in every human being sometimes a longing to kick over the traces. He's been in a groove too long an' he wants to get out an' bust up something. Morality, politics, religion—it takes men different ways, but most of them feel the urge whether they do anything about it or not. Now I'm not in physical shape, either way you take that, to go out on a Don Juan spree, or a crusade or even a binge, so what I do is bust every rule of grammar I ever knew, when I feel like it, see? If I want to split an infinitive I split it if you can hear the crack a mile away. God, I've been careful over my years as a Judge about infinitives, *an'* verbs, *an'* adjectives an' all the rest of it. Now I'm in a carefully calculated *revolt* an' I get the damnedest lot of relief from it."

"Well, *set!*" the Judge repeated now, and Gavin dropped into the other wicker chair.

Suddenly the older man leaned his huge bulk forward on the iron railing and peered into the street. Two young girls were passing, giggling brightly and swaying in the way best suited to set off their sinuous charms. The Judge watched them out of sight and then turned to Gavin.

"Temptin', ain't they?" he drawled.

Gavin laughed. "Well, I guess that was nature's general intention."

"You just bet it was," agreed the Judge. "An' whether you've thought of this much or not, it ain't the *male* that's the real seducer. It's the young female with her little breasts bobbin' an' her little hindies swingin' an' her face like dawn breakin' in the sky. Whether she knows it or not, *she's* the one . . ."

"That launches the ships and burns the towers. I know. And offers the apple," Gavin added grinning, "if we care to change the classical allusion."

"Yep!" said the Judge. "You got it the first time. Well, how's that little daughter of Eve you have out at your house? God, she's a beauty. I'd never insult her by callin' her *pretty*. It's more than that, Gavin. She's got what happens by accident once in ten thousand times or so. By the way, never deny the place of *accident* in the great life process, when you're doin' your thinkin', my boy. It's important. Well, what are you goin' to do with little Rosie?"

5

"She'd be mad at you for calling her Rosie. How do you mean, what am I going to *do* with her?"

"Well, she's a Senior in your college now, ain't she? Boys buzzin' round her I spose?"

"Oh, yes."

"Any one in particular?"

"The Scott boy."

"Umhm. A little too sporty as far as I can make out."

"I agree. I'm not too happy about it. But she's twenty-one. I can't play the Victorian father. I wouldn't want to estrange her, we've always been pretty close. When I think how upset Cecily and I were when we found we were going to have her . . . You see I was studying for my Master's when we got married, on nothing flat. Cecily got a job and I worked like the devil. The night I had my degree we really celebrated, throwing caution to the winds, financially and otherwise. A little later we knew we were going to have a baby. I made Cecily stop work and I got a high school job and gave up going on for my Doctorate. I guess I've told you this, haven't I?"

"Just some of it. But what are you doing now about your Doctor's?"

"Not a thing. I've given up till I can take

a whole year off and concentrate. I can't study and teach college English and pull my weight at home at the same time. I've been saving up again. Cecily's been wonderful about it. She seems to feel it was entirely her fault each time we've had a baby. You see Rose was such a darling from the beginning we hadn't the heart to . . . Well, I hadn't meant to tell you but I really think I may be able to swing it by another year if no other crisis comes up. As you know, we've had our share."

"If you weren't such a damned pigheaded, independent cuss and would let . . ."

"Now, now, we've been over that. Well, I've got to go. Cecily says all the overcooked dinners we've ever eaten in Marsden have been due to you. But she always wants me to give you her love anyway."

"Give her mine. Nicest woman I ever met. Well, get along to her now an' leave an old bachelor to dree his weird as best he can. You're a great comfort to me, Gavin."

"That goes both ways," the younger man said with his quick smile, and set off up the remaining slope of the street.

The houses grew more spacious here, wide-spread pale bricks and clapboards, indicating comfort without ostentation.

There was, indeed, a great deal of money in Marsden. It was the kind of quiet-moving, deep-rooted town where many families lived for generations, giving it permanence and a social distinction while their fortunes in coal or natural gas formed an unobtrusive background to their lives. Rather as elegant clothes are worn by the initiate with casualness.

The abodes of wealth were for the most part on the perimeter of Marsden so that acreage could surround the houses; there were, however, a few dignified stone and brick dwellings where luxury lived, by choice, in town. And in between all of these were the houses, mostly frame, of what might be called the yeomanry, the substantial class of professional men, the tradesmen, dealers in all manner of commodities from harvesters for the wide farming community surrounding to dry goods and groceries. And on the very outer social fringe, hanging on by their heels, as it were, lived those who had never even dreamed of luxury and who had only a minimum of comfort. So went Marsden as did many other towns like it across the country.

Gavin had reached the very end of Main Street now, where surprisingly enough it ended in a hayfield at one side and a thin bit of woods on the other. Of course the march of progress would soon take both these, but as long as they lasted they were there to enjoy. So was the rather large, yellow frame house just beyond the woods, with its gingerbread cornices and wide piazza. It had been built in Victorian style, but had fallen upon the evil days of unappreciative renters before Gavin and Cecily saw it when they first came house-hunting to Marsden. They went through it then in utter silence except for the fluent remarks of the real estate agent. It spoke to them, however, as houses do. It faced the east with a far view of the Blue Ridge from the living room windows; it had clinging to it, even with its shabby walls, a faint aroma of past aristocracy; it was big enough for their growing family; and there was a wide lawn outside with maple trees shading it and pines and beeches at the back. When they had made the rounds Gavin and Cecily looked at each other and smiled. He used then the very words he had spoken when they had decided to be married.

"Let's call it settled," he said.

The house had done well by them as they had by it. The fundamentals were good: the furnace worked well, as did the bathroom;

the roof was sound. Little by little Gavin had painted and papered the walls that first summer; Cecily had made slipcovers for the living room furniture. In a little half second-hand, half antique shop on a back street they had found some surprise treasures which, as the proprietor explained, had come from the homes of "the big bugs." Bought with little cash but much discrimination, cleaned or waxed and placed to advantage in the yellow house, they gave a touch of elegance the owners could not have afforded first-hand.

"What if one day later on we should get to know some of the important families here!" Cecily said anxiously. "Imagine if a woman should come to call and recognize her old table or rug? I'd die of embarrassment."

"Not a bit," Gavin had encouraged her stoutly. "The people who bought these things in the first place *liked* them, didn't they, or they wouldn't have chosen them. Well, now we like them too, so that just shows we have congenial tastes."

Gavin had reached the edge of the lawn now and, as he often did, gave a wild whoop to announce his arrival. The sound brought immediate results. Bruce, now eighteen and a duplicate of Gavin himself, came from the backyard, and Ian, a nearly as tall sixteen, from his lawn mower on the side. Cecily herself, with little Cissie beside her, ran down the front steps. There was always a warm meeting at the end of the day between Gavin and his wife.

"I will *never*," he had told her after their marriage, "condescend to a peck on the cheek no matter who's looking." And he never had.

"Say," Bruce began, "that was a lousy exam you gave us today, Pop."

"Ha! Caught you out, did I? Well, you just put a little more time on your English, my lad. I'm known as a hard marker."

"I've heard *that* before," the boy retorted, grinning.

"Come on up to the porch and give me all the news—if there's time before dinner," he said, looking apologetically at Cecily. "I did stop a few minutes with the Judge."

"You and your *minutes!* You're good for an hour when you stop there. Dinner is practically done. I'd better get back to it and you all get ready. I had the *loveliest* afternoon, Gavin."

"Oh, I forgot. This was the tea party at Mrs. Wilson's, wasn't it? And you had a good time?"

"Simply wonderful. I'm all set up. Tell you later."

"Where's Rose?" Gavin asked.

"Oh, she went straight up to her room to finish some work, I guess."

"She ought to be out in the fresh air now after all day in school."

He went into the hall and called from the foot of the stairs. "Rose! Rose!" And then, "Ros . . . *ie!*"

The girl appeared at the door of her room. "Oh, Daddy, please don't ever call me that. It makes me feel like a six-year-old. I hate it."

"O.K. I'll only use it in emergencies. What are you doing up there this lovely afternoon?"

"Oh, I had a paper to finish. Thought I'd get it done when I was in the mood."

"Well, come on down now and get your lungs full of fresh air before dinner. We breathe enough dust and chalk all day to call for a little ozone."

He went on up to his own room to freshen up and change to a smoking jacket which Cecily had bought for him some years ago. "I feel like a landed gentleman when I get this on," he often said laughingly, but he still made a pleased little ceremony of

12

wearing it every night. He could hear Cissie, their youngest, a little seven-year-old sprite, laughing and calling to her brothers below, who teased her unmercifully and worshiped her all the while. He listened for Rose. She had a voice like a lark and the house usually held echoes of her songs. Come to think of it she hadn't been singing much lately and he had missed it. He wondered, uneasily, if she was falling in love with the Scott boy. He belonged to the *Establishment,* as it were, lived on one of the largest estates bordering the town, drove to college in a red sports car and did practically no work when he got there. Gavin knew he was attending Marsden because he couldn't get into one of the larger colleges. Even his entrance at Marsden *might* have been aided by the fact that his father, Loren Scott, was a trustee and was expected to contribute heavily to the new library, being planned for some years now. In addition to money and position young Scott had good looks and, it had to be admitted, a most engaging personality. He could charm a bird off a tree, Gavin was thinking now. Had he charmed Rose? With all his heart, he hoped not. The boy never looked you straight in the eye.

As they sat down to dinner Gavin glanced

around the table with satisfaction, forgetting his fears momentarily. Across from him was Cecily, still lovely to look upon in her first forties. The various crises of their married life: Bruce's desperate pneumonia, Ian's one-time shattered leg; little Cissie's premature arrival which left both her and her mother near death's door—all these and others had seemed but to point up Cecily's natural resilience. So she smiled back at him now as she had that faraway day on the woods path when he knew he must marry her. Bruce was a tall, handsome blond lad, a Junior in college; Ian in his last year in high school, tall also but dark—a Black Scot, his father called him—with only an almost imperceptible limp from the long ago sledding disaster; little Cissie was going to be her mother's own daughter: the same honey-colored eyes, the curling hair, the bright smile; and Rose! Even his father's heart versed in long familiarity always quickened as he looked upon his eldest child. For as the Judge had remarked, she had beauty, that subtle, evanescent quality which no mere definition of features can describe. There was the pure oval of the face, the perfect nose, the long dark-fringed violet eyes, the curving red lips—but nature's *accident* had added something more.

"Well," Gavin began, as he carved the meat, "since your mother has had the most exciting day, probably, let's have her tell the news first."

Cecily leaned forward a little with her smile encompassing them all. "Oh, I'm dying to tell you about it. Though I suddenly realize it may not sound glamorous to you at all. Of course the Wilson house is the most pretentious and the most beautiful in Marsden and I've been there before to committee meetings and large occasions but today is the first time I've been invited to an intimate social affair. Mrs. Wilson entertains very seldom, and never for cocktails as she doesn't like them. So, this was *tea* in the magnificent library with a fire going and the tea table, just shining with silver, drawn up in front of it like something out of an English novel. And of course flowers everywhere. There were only eight of us and Mrs. Wilson managed without any effort at all to direct the conversation as she poured the tea. She is really old, I imagine, but she's still handsome and witty and very intelligent and . . ."

She paused. No one, she knew, except Gavin was really interested in her recital.

"Well, anyway," she ended quickly, "it was all surprisingly gay and stimulating and pleasant and I enjoyed it."

"Good!" Gavin said. "I think Mrs. Wilson is charming. She bears out the French opinion that women grow more attractive as they get older. I've noticed that myself—at close range," he added slyly.

This brought a laugh from the boys as Cecily blushed.

"You'd know Pop was up on the poets," Bruce said, "since he's so good at making pretty speeches."

"He's good at everything," Cecily answered. "Well, come on now. I've told *my* news."

"Nothing exciting in my day," Gavin said, "except that I looked over the plans for the new library again. The architect left them in Dr. Waring's office. I like them immensely. How I want to see that library built! It would give Marsden a new look, and no mistake, aside from its cultural value. All we need," he added, "is the money."

"Say," Ian said suddenly as he passed his plate for a second helping, "the darnedest thing happened in French class today. You know Betsy Hallam, don't you, Rose?"

"Yes, slightly."

"Well, when she got up to recite she turned white as a sheet and keeled over in the aisle, just as if she was dead. It scared the liver out of all of us. Mam'selle phoned to the office and the principal and the nurse came and they carried her out, but gee, it was *something!* She's all right *now,* we heard, but what on earth would make her do that, Mother?"

"Oh, any number of things," Cecily said. "The beginning of a virus, maybe. There's a lot of flu around. And maybe *lack of sleep.* And that reminds me I want you all in bed in decent time tonight! There was a girl in college," she went on reminiscently, "who always fainted when the room got too hot. We got used to it and someone was always putting a window up."

"And what's the matter with *you,*" Ian said, looking across at his sister. "You look about as white as Betsy did."

"Don't be an idiot," Rose returned. "That's my new face powder. It's supposed to make me look ethereal."

"It makes you look as if you'd stuck your head in the flour barrel," Ian came back with brotherly candor.

"Now, now," Gavin said mildly. "Did you rehearse today, Rose?"

17

"Yes, and it really didn't go too badly for the first time with the orchestra. I still think it was crazy to choose an old thing like 'The Student Prince' when we could have done something really snappy and avant garde. But that's Marsden for you! The funny thing, though, is that it's *so* old none of the kids have ever seen it. So it's all new to them. And of course it makes a big cast possible."

"Who has the male lead?"

Rose sniffed. "Honest Abe. He's got the best voice in college so they practically had to pick him. But his acting! A wooden Indian would be more . . ."

Bruce broke in. "I think you girls are mean to call him that. He knows it and he hates it. He's tall and not so good looking and of course there is the name, but that's all the resemblance. He's a nice guy. The fellows all like him."

"Abe Williams?" Gavin asked, with interest. "He's got a brilliant mind, that boy."

"Well, I only hope he limbers up for the show. I give you my word it's like playing up to a fence post. And if he'd *only* get some new clothes."

"Don't blame him. I heard they were as

poor as Job's turkey. They live on a little farm back here somewhere," Bruce said, "and Abe walks nearly three miles every day to college and back."

Cecily suddenly raised her hand. "Now, everybody, we come to the real climax of the dinner. Cissie wanted to wait until dessert for her great announcement. The ice cream is now on, so go ahead, Cissie!"

The little girl looked around the table, her eyes dancing. "I got an A in reading," she said.

There was general wild acclaim. So far Cissie had not taken to the academic life as her brothers and sister had always done, so now she accepted the tribute for her unusual triumph graciously and beamed upon them all. Ian deftly wound his napkin into a crown and set it on her head, and there was more applause.

"Good girl!" Gavin said. "Now keep it up! We're very proud of you!"

The meal ended as usual with chatter and laughter. Cecily went to the kitchen where Cissie, in spite of possible breakage, was to dry the dishes. The boys went out to work on the car and Gavin strolled over to the bookshelves in the living room to look for a volume he needed. Rose had gone quietly through to the hall. On impulse Gavin followed her.

"Rose," he said, as she turned at the stairs, "there's something I'd like to say to you and I'm not sure I should. You're old enough to make your own decisions, but I am still older. So I feel I must offer my advice for what it's worth. I know you've been dating Lester Scott a good deal. I know how attractive he is but I don't know whether under this charm he has the sound qualities that are worthy of you. My advice is to go slow. *Slowly,*" he added with a small grin. "Get to know him very well before you let your feelings become involved . . ."

He stopped, for suddenly the tears were running down Rose's cheeks and she was starting hastily up the stairs.

"Now I've done it!" Gavin muttered to himself as he went back to the bookshelves. "If she's really fallen in love with this boy what I said will make her unhappy. I hope it won't make her mad at me. Oh, it's the very devil, sometimes, to be the father of a daughter."

He sat down on the sofa, thinking. If there was anything serious between Rose and young Scott there would be for her the background of wealth and luxury to which, strangely, he had hardly given a thought. What a perfect, what a fairy-tale setting for Rose's beauty! But he slowly shook his head. He's no good, that fellow, he thought. I'm sure of it. And the money wouldn't make up for that.

There was another problem in connection with Lester which had been half brought to light that very afternoon by Devereux, the history professor. He was a wise, witty and, according to Gavin's opinion, a completely unambitious man, who would be quite content to teach there the rest of his life. Gavin not only hoped for a "bigger tent" someday, but was always planning for Marsden's growth and improvement while he was there. The new library, for example, had been his idea and he had worked in season and out for its fulfillment. Dr. Waring had finally caught fire and now the architect's plans lay in his office for all the faculty to see and the trustees to pass upon later. Gavin's heart leaped at the thought of what had been accomplished so far even though so much more was needed.

Devereux had sauntered up to him as he was walking across the campus and begun abruptly in his usual drawl.

"And what about our fair-feathered young

friend, Scott?" he asked.

"What about him?"

"Is he passing English?"

"Not by a long shot. Even with super-human effort he couldn't possibly make up the work now. I've talked to him. I've offered to help him. But it's been no go. What's he doing in history?"

"Nothing," said Devereux. "With a great big N and a large curl of the g's tail. I repeat, *Nothing*. But we may have to give or take a little before we're done, Gavin."

"There's a point beyond which we can't either give or take."

"That is, *you* can't. You're a Scotsman. To the day you die black will be black and white will be white and never the twain shall meet. Now me, I'm two-thirds French. *So!* First of all I'm practical. Second, I've been born with a genius for compromise. Oh, we may not run into any real problem about this. But apropos of that, the best advice I ever heard about how to act in a crisis was given by our old family doctor."

"What was that?" Gavin asked curiously.

" 'Trust in God and keep the bowels open.' Well, good-night, my noble sir. As Shakespeare would say, 'I can smell honor a mile away, though I have it not myself.' "

And with a courtly wave he turned toward his car.

Gavin had gone on, chuckling. He was very fond of Devereux. They had many a sound and scintillating discussion when the latter was in the mood for serious talk. Most of the time his wit, his satire, his "original" Shakespearean quotations skivered along the surface like rabbits running from pursuing hounds.

As he sat now on the sofa Gavin was considering what effect it would have upon Rose if Lester did not graduate. She must know he was failing though he might have covered up the danger ahead. As to himself, he had made a point of never discussing his students' work in the family even as a doctor would not divulge his patients' ailments. But Rose had a high respect for scholarship. Perhaps Lester's defection in this line would in itself make a break between them. With a sigh he turned to his book.

When he and Cecily were alone in their bedroom that night she turned from her dressing table, looking absurdly young in her low-cut nightgown.

"Gavin," she said, "I'm afraid Rose and Lester Scott have broken up. I've caught her crying twice, and you know they haven't gone out together for two weeks and he hasn't called. The trouble is he's too attractive. Other boys will seem tame by comparison. I must confess he's sort of won me over too when he's been here. Then there's all the money. I hate myself for thinking about it but I do. It would be so perfect for Rose. Why have you never liked the boy?''

"Well," Gavin said slowly, "I have him in class and can study him a little. I don't approve of his bringing up. Only child, mother dead, father doting on him and denying him nothing, it seems. I think he's a spoiled, arrogant, unprincipled young man. I'm sure he believes that the Scott money and position would admit him to heaven or anywhere else without further qualifications. So, as far as I'm concerned I'm very relieved indeed if they've broken up. And another thing," he added.

"What, Gavin?"

"I don't believe Bruce likes him. I overheard something one night some time ago. Rose was coming down the stairs, ready to go out, and Bruce was apparently waiting for her in the hall. They didn't know I was within earshot. He said, 'Take it easy, Rose, will you?' And she said, 'Mind your own business.' But you can see that Bruce didn't like the set-up.''

Cecily sighed. ''Of course at her age she'll get over it, and I'll forget my wild dreams of seeing her mistress of the Scott mansion and queen of Marsden society.''

It was when Cecily was almost asleep that Gavin spoke again.

''Darling,'' he said, hesitatingly, ''have you ever spoken to Rose—oh, you know —mother-daughter confidences about, well, about *things?*''

She gave a drowsy chuckle. ''Oh, you really are behind the times if you're thinking of the 'facts of life' business. She probably knows as much as I do. More than I did at her age. *Of course* I've discussed my own views of manners and morals in general as plainly as I can, but that's about all a mother can do these days. She's knowledgeable, dear, and fine. Don't worry.''

It rained in the night and the air next morning was delicately clean and fragrant with spring. From the beech trees at the back of the lot the doves were giving their muted mourning call. Gavin was particularly fond of this sound and as soon as he was dressed hurried down to the garden where he could hear it better and examine the first up-

25

springing bulbs. Next to his family and his work he loved his garden. As Cecily always said he had better than a green thumb, he had a whole green hand, the true gardener's touch. Because of this there were beds of flowers from spring until fall down either side of the back lawn and a charming circle of all-white bloom bordered by carefully laid broken flagstones at the back. Focal point, Gavin called it.

His fond hobby had brought him friends as well as information. Early in his stay in Marsden he had driven past the Wilson garden and, getting out of the car, stood looking over the massed beauty of the beds. An old man, seeing his expression of delight, left his wheelbarrow and came over to the hedge.

"Would you like to come in an' have a look 'round?"

Gavin had gone in and in a short time he and Home were on pleasant footing.

"Would you have a little drop of Scotch in your blood by any chance," the old man asked. "From your name you ought."

"All of it," Gavin answered. "I was born there."

"Fine!" said Home. "You're *in,* man, then, for the Scotch are the best gardeners in the world." He raised an imaginary glass. "Here's tae us. Wha's like us?"

Mrs. Wilson had come out with her basket and shears and Gavin had been drawn to her at once.

"Oh," she said cordially, "I've heard of you. You're the new English professor at the College, aren't you? And you've bought the Holcomb house. It's been a nice one in its day. I'm glad you're in it. I must meet your wife. Let me send her some flowers."

He had come away warmed by friendliness and with Home's promise to look in after work and give him advice on his planting. Over the years the garden interest had proved an open sesame to more of the large estates and their owners. A most pleasant bond of acquaintance, Gavin thought, though he and Cecily had always allowed it to come about naturally.

He peered now at the beds. The perennials were beginning to show their heads, the daffodils were in bud and down beneath the trees were clouds of slim gold and blue chalices springing delicately but strongly from the still cold earth. Gavin smiled and since no one was within hearing began to repeat to himself an old favorite:

> *. . .When far down some glade*
> *Of the great world's burning*
> *One soft flame upturning*
> *Seems to his discerning*
> Crocus *in the shade.*

He looked across to the wooded hills beyond the town. Every possible shade of new green was there with a few dull browns amongst them to temper their exuberant freshness. Delaying winter in the arms of spring, he was thinking.

"Breakfast, Gavin," came a call from the kitchen door. "Come on."

It was part of Cecily's New England inheritance that she believed in hearty breakfasts for her family. Even though it made her get up in the mornings earlier than would otherwise have been necessary, often with a face a little pale from a late night's reading, she would not listen to Gavin's remonstrance.

"I can nap in the afternoon," she would always say, "but I simply must see you all start off for the day well fed."

The children had grown up with this habit and the boys especially took to it with zest. Sometimes Rose demurred as if in fright. "I'll *gain*, Mother, on a breakfast like this."

Cecily was always calmly adamant. "You can eat a lighter lunch then. Breakfast is the most important."

So they all sat down each morning to cereal (except on pancake day), bacon and eggs or fried mush and maple syrup or any other variations Cecily could devise. This morning there were muffins with homemade peach jam and scrambled eggs. From the quantities consumed Cecily knew her efforts were appreciated; there was little con- versation, however, for time always pressed. When the meal was over Gavin got his briefcase and joined the children at the car. The day before Cecily had needed it to go to the tea at Mrs. Wilson's but now they could drive. Cecily saw them off with a kiss for each. "As though you never expected to see us again!" Bruce often teased her. But he and Ian, even at their ages now, accepted the caresses as they did the hearty breakfasts as part of the pattern of the day ordained by their mother.

Gavin dropped little Cissie off at her school, then Ian, which left the three of them to proceed to the Marsden campus. His own thoughts were busy with the coming operetta.

"About Abe Williams, Rose," he began,

"you say he's not much of an actor?"

"That," said Rose sharply, "is your greatest understatement."

"Miss Matthews is directing?"

"Yes."

"Is she doing a good job?"

"Fair."

"Has she ever had you and Abe rehearse by yourselves since you're the two principals?"

Rose made a sound like a groan. "Oh, I couldn't stand that. He *obnoxes* me, as the boys say. The trouble with him is he has no feeling, no imagination."

"But that's not true. He's got plenty of both. You forget I have a way of knowing him that probably no one else has. I read his themes. There ought to be some way to get him out of his shell."

"Well, anyone can try it for all I care," Rose responded, and her voice suddenly was flat with all its usual lilt gone out of it.

She's hurt, Gavin thought sadly, *and Lester Scott's not worth it. But the streams of the heart must run their own course.*

They had reached the rather imposing stone gates now which marked the beginning of the academic grounds. Although the institution was rated somewhat condescendingly in certain manuals as a small co-ed, denominational college, there was one feature of which it could be proud. Founded nearly a hundred years before when acreage was plentiful and to spare, the campus, beautifully wooded and kept with care, stretched for nearly a mile on three sides. Because of the beauty of this, many parents coming from a distance to look the place over mentally decided to enroll their sons and daughters there before they had gone much beyond the stone gates. Old Main, as the first of the buildings was always called, had withstood the years well, though inside its heavy wooden stairs had hollows from the many young feet which had trodden them. On the outside, however, its age had been covered with grace, as an ivy planted long ago by a graduating class had now spread its green over all the front brick. A rather large cupola, probably the long-ago architect's pride, added a certain venerable dignity.

Behind Old Main were the old and new dormitories, the Science Building, the combined athletic and auditorium edifice, and West Hall, given over entirely to classrooms.

Gavin parked the car, gave a cheerful "good luck" to Bruce and Rose and made his way around the winding, wooded walk to the modern three-story stone building where his work was done. His mind was still considering the problem of the operetta and Abe Williams. Rose was definitely wrong about the boy. There was not only a fine mind there but, as revealed in his papers, a certain emotional fire, or perhaps as of now, just the capacity for it. Behind his shy and awkward exterior there was soul enough if it could somehow be released. Gavin sat at his desk and pondered since it was still ten minutes before his first class. All at once he drew from an envelope in his briefcase a small clipping. It was a poem he had seen once in the *New York Times* under their section of Queries and Answers, one which with all his wide knowledge of literature he had never come across before. He had culled it immediately and put it with other little unexpected "finds" to present to his classes at appropriate times. He read it over now and his response to it was as great as when he had first seen it. He had an idea that Abe Williams would have the same feeling. Well, it was worth the experiment.

When Abe came into the classroom, always a little early in spite of his three-mile walk, Gavin spoke to him.

"Would you stay a little while after school this afternoon, Abe? There's something I'd like to talk over with you."

"Why . . . why yes," the boy answered at once, but his face fell.

When they were alone together at four, Gavin went straight to the point.

"How's the operetta going, Abe?"

"I thought that was likely what you wanted to see me about. I'm no good in it. I'd get out of it if I could. I can sing all right, I guess. That's the Welsh in me. My parents came from Wales. But even in the main song Miss Matthews says I don't put any feeling in it. And my lines are awful. R—R—Rose doesn't say anything but I can tell by the way she looks she's disgusted. After rehearsal I feel as though I could drown myself. And the thing is when they picked me for the part I was sort of . . . well, I mean the way I am . . . I mean I was pretty happy."

There was a pathos in the boy's voice and attitude that went to Gavin's heart.

"Well now," he began, "let's see what we can do about this. I used to be pretty keen on dramatics when I was in college. And the first thing you have to learn of course is to forget yourself and *be* the character you're portraying. Not just pretend. That's no good. That shows through every time. You've got to live and breathe and *be* the person in the play. You've heard of a man falling over his own feet, I suppose.''

The boy grinned slightly.

"Well, that's what you're doing. You're falling over Abe Williams. Now you've got to forget him at rehearsals. Leave him at home. *You are the young Student Prince.* And right now, just for practice in getting out of your own skin into another's, I want you to read me a little poem. Will you?''

"I'll . . . I'll try," he stammered.

"I found this by chance," Gavin said, drawing out the slip from its envelope. "I had never seen it before all through the years and it somehow moved me deeply. Read it over a couple of times or more to yourself until you get the feel of it, then I want you to do it aloud.''

Abe took the small clipping and Gavin watched him as his eyes scanned it. There was first on his face a mere interest, and then a deeper expression as color came slowly into his cheeks. It was some time before he looked up.

"What do you think of it?" Gavin asked.

"It's beautiful."

"Do you understand it?"

"Oh, yes."

"Now I want you to get the picture. As the title says, it's an Arab love song. It is night on the desert. The camels are kneeling, asleep, their shadows 'troubling' the moonlight, as the poet says. The young Arab himself is standing there under the stars looking across to the tents of his sweetheart's tribe. He is pouring out his very soul in love for her. You, now, *are that young Bedouin,* as you read. Go ahead."

Abe's speaking voice also had the rich timbre of his Welsh inheritance. He began quietly.

> *The hunchèd camels of the night*
> *Trouble the bright*
> *And silver waters of the moon.*
> *The Maiden of the Moon will soon*
> *Through Heaven stray and sing,*
> *Star gathering.*

Gavin's tense ear caught the crescendo.

> *Now while the dark about our loves*
> *   is strewn,*
> *Light of my dark, blood of my heart,*
> *   O come!*

35

And night will catch her breath up, and
  be dumb.

Leave thy father, leave thy mother
And thy brother;
Leave the black tents of thy tribe apart!
Am I not thy father and thy brother,
And thy mother?
And thou—what needest with thy tribe's
  black tents
Who hast the red pavilion of my heart?

The passionate cry of the last two lines came through! Gavin drew a quick breath and felt his eyes misty. The boy stood with a frightened look as though he found himself naked. Gavin rose and smiled into his startled face.

"You've done it, Abe. You've crossed the barrier between your own personality and another's. Now, you can do it any time. You can do it in your play. Don't you feel a kind of power in yourself? The ability to let yourself go, emotionally? You swept me along. Think what you can do to an audience."

"That might be harder."

"Easier," Gavin assured him. "There's always a transference from the audience to you. And vice versa. Well, I don't think you have to worry any more about rehearsals. When's the next one?"

"Tomorrow afternoon."

"Good! Give them the surprise of their lives, for you can do it."

"I wonder," Abe said, fingering the small clipping, "if I could borrow this for a few days to . . . to practice on it. Seems to loosen up my wheels somehow."

"Of course. I'd like it back but keep it as long as you wish. When you return it I'll type you a copy. Well, good luck now. We'd both better be on our way."

Abe put out his hand awkwardly. "Professor McAllister, I've often wanted to tell you what it's meant to me to be in your classes, but I never had the nerve. And now, your helping me with this . . . well, I can't thank you enough."

"Why, that's all right, Abe. I've enjoyed having you in class very much indeed. Your themes often lifted my spirits when I had a good many stodgy ones to go over. As to your reading now, I got a bigger thrill out of that than you did, I'm sure. Well, so long!"

Gavin swung along the campus walks with his easy stride, hastened by a fine sense of accomplishment. He always walked back at the end of the day, first because he enjoyed the exercise and second because the time of his leaving was uncertain. Bruce and Rose would now be home in the car. He was relieved to see that the Judge was not on the lookout for him because the hour was already late. He decided to keep the secret of his rendezvous with Abe. Tomorrow night at dinner he would inquire casually about the rehearsal and discover how Rose had been affected by it, for he was sure there would be real news to tell.

By the following afternoon, however, the matter of the operetta had been driven far from his mind. A brief note had been left on each teacher's desk that morning saying that Dr. Waring was calling a most important faculty meeting in his office at four o'clock that day. Gavin gave it small thought as the hours passed. Waring's meetings were all "of the utmost importance." This probably would be, however, since the architect's plans for the library were yet to be discussed; also suggestions as to how more money could be raised. As he moved about his classroom, occasionally he allowed his eyes to rest with pleasure upon the broad greensward where the new building would ultimately stand. His heart always rose at thought of the library. The dream would someday be a reality, though it still might take years to fulfill it.

He was the last to enter Dr. Waring's office at four since he had forgotten some papers and had to go back for them before the janitor locked the classroom. Gavin spoke a bit breathlessly in apology and took the last empty chair next to the president himself. Dr. Waring rose to his feet, a paper in his hand. He was a small man in every respect, Gavin thought, always trying to make up for it by earnest efforts to impress. The top of his head was bald and with the aid of his barber the side hair was long enough to comb over it. This was somehow repellent to Gavin who didn't like the man in any case.

Dr. Waring now began to speak, an undercurrent of excitement in his tone, as he adjusted his glasses with an habitual motion.

"I have called you in at this time to read you a letter that reached me only late yesterday afternoon. I felt I could not wait another day before sharing with you my own elation at its contents."

He glanced around the expectant circle as though to prolong the suspense for a moment and then went on.

"It comes from Mr. Loren Scott, Chairman of our Board of Trustees and perhaps the most affluent man in town. It reads as follows:

DEAR DR. WARING:

After careful consideration I have decided to make a contribution of $150,000 toward the building of the new library, to be given on the day my son graduates from Marsden. As I watch him cross the stage to receive his diploma it will be one of the great moments of my life. This gift will be a father's appreciation of that moment. I would suggest that you and the faculty (whom you may wish to tell) will respect this as a confidence so that the announcement will have the element of surprise on Commencement Day.

With warmest regards and gratitude for what you have done for our college, I am

Very truly yours,
LOREN SCOTT"

Dr. Waring looked around him at the faces expressing variously amazement, pleasure and something of shock, while subdued comments began. He raised a finger.

"There is something we as a faculty will of course have to discuss in connection with this munificent offer." He cleared his throat. "There is the matter of Lester Scott's . . . ah . . . classroom standing. Now, I wish to make this observation. It may be necessary for us to be over lenient in respect to his grades. But consider this. At the moment we are at a standstill in our fund-raising for the library. The money which Mr. Scott so generously offers will make it possible to start on the building at once, if the architect's plans are approved. Now in accepting this gift we will be weighing not the merits or demerits of one boy. We'll be providing a much needed cultural center for hundreds, as the years go on, thousands of students. My earnest hope is that you will now in your own minds seek for the greatest good of the greatest number and act accordingly. I will call upon you each in turn for your reaction to this letter. Dr. Foster, you are first."

The lady addressed was a tall, thin female whose rather lengthy nose had a tendency to twitch under emotion, giving her the universal nickname of *Bunny*. She had taught in the Ancient Languages department for years, perhaps, as Gavin wickedly wondered sometimes, because her brother-in-law was on the Board of Trustees. She was now definitely a-twitch and one might say, embarrassed.

"Dr. Waring, you have given us guidance in what would . . . I mean there is a question . . . I should say rather a problem involved which you have certainly . . . I mean you have given a definite clarity to the situation. My vote—if that is what you are asking for—will be in line with your own suggestion."

"Thank you, Dr. Foster, for your gracious words."

He went on around the circle. There was a good deal of clearing of throats and fumbling for appropriate phraseology, but there was no dissenting voice. When it came Devereux's turn Gavin met his eyes squarely and received what was remarkably close to a wink, covered up immediately.

"Ah," said he in a somber tone, "this matter of ethical decisions is the most difficult in life. Yet how aptly Shakespeare has expressed it: *For oft the* must not *doth become the* must *when hard necessity demands it.* In this case I feel we are faced not only by strong but very pleasant necessity in accepting Mr. Scott's fine offer."

There were a few more teachers to be heard from, several repetitions of the greatest good of the greatest number, and one or two mentions of the end justifying the means in a compromise. At last there was only Gavin left. Dr. Waring by this time was smiling broadly. It was evident he had feared more discussion.

"And now, Professor McAllister, we have reached you."

"Do I understand, Doctor, that you wish my honest opinion of this letter you have just read to us?" His Scottish chin was set like iron.

"I most certainly do," the President answered unctuously.

"Then here it is." Gavin's voice was clear as ice. "I think this letter is the subtlest, most diabolical piece of blackmail I have ever heard of in my life."

A sort of audible shudder could be felt in the room as Dr. Waring's face changed from red to purple and then most dangerously to white.

"I believe," he spat out the words, "that Professor McAllister will wish to withdraw that statement."

"Not at all," Gavin said. "I only wish to expand upon it, as, since I've made it, I think I have a right to do. The way I see it is this," he went on, addressing his colleagues while Dr. Waring seemed unable to speak further at the moment. "We all know that Lester Scott hasn't passed a single subject or tried to do so. His father has been informed along the way of the boy's failure. Now this letter in essence says, 'If you, the faculty, will pass the boy anyhow, hand him a diploma he has not earned, I will give you one hundred and fifty thousand dollars. If you won't do this'—well, I think the inference is clear that we don't get the money."

The room was still as death as Gavin went on.

"Now I think it is safe to say that no one of you wants that library more than I do. I have worked in season and out of season for it, perhaps harder than anyone else has. But I would rather have Marsden lose that library or wait for years to get it than have this faculty—all of us—do a dishonest thing. All the Senior class knows Scott has failed. What will they think of us, how can they respect us, if they see him get a diploma like the rest of them and hear the gift read out on

Commencement Day? I think, sir," he added turning to the President, "that it is more important for Marsden College to keep its integrity and never allow itself to be *bought,* than for it to have the new library. That is all I have to say."

Dr. Waring still seemed to find speech difficult. Then he said slowly, "I cannot adequately express my feeling of shock over this most unwarranted interpretation of the situation before us . . ."

Another voice was suddenly raised. It came from Dr. Schneider, head of the science department. He was dark, rotund and friendly, peering through thick-lensed glasses as though always squinting through a microscope. He spoke with a slight German accent. "Dr. Waring," he went on, "if I may change my original statement I will now concur with Professor McAllister. In my work in the field of science it is even more incumbent on me than on the rest of you that I should be always honest."

Dr. Waring gave him a glassy stare. "The meeting is dismissed," he said, "for the present. We will convene later." And he turned to the door of his private office and disappeared.

Gavin got out as fast as possible, avoiding

speech with anyone. He did grip Schneider's hand as he passed him. Out on the walk, however, Devereux caught up with him.

"Well, my noble sir," he began, "don't say I didn't warn you."

"You dog!" Gavin burst out. "You and your bogus Shakespeare quotations! You make me sick."

"Well now," Devereux responded mildly, with a grin, "I thought that 'quote' was pretty clever to be thought up on the spur of the moment. You know, Gavin, I'd bet you dollars to doughnuts that I could write the act of a so-called Shakespearean play and fool even you!"

"I've been fooled enough by you for one day," Gavin answered tartly. "Why didn't you back me up? I'm ashamed of you. Good old Schneider!" he added.

"Oh, I can tell you why I didn't back you up. First, it would have been dangerous, and second it would have been futile."

Gavin stopped in his tracks. "What do you mean, *dangerous?*"

"Did it never occur to you that the Great White Papa Waring might lop off a head or two if he was opposed? He wants that library as fast as it can be built. Not for Marsden, but so he can be alive and able to read his name on a plaque and give the dedication speech and all that jazz. He might just need to be in a hurry at that. I thought he was going to have a stroke when you were talking.''

''You actually think I could lose my job over what I said?'' Gavin asked slowly.

''Oh, I doubt if it would come to that but knowing Waring's disposition and his devious ways I don't think it would do any harm to throw him a little sop . . .''

''Which I don't intend to do. As to what I said being futile, I simply can't believe . . .''

''Gavin, sometimes you don't show Scotch common sense. Do you for one moment think that Waring and the trustees themselves will throw one hundred and fifty thousand dollars over their shoulders just because one lousy kid hasn't done any work worth speaking of, all year? They'll get around that, you'll see.''

He paused and squinted up to the sky where the spring sunset shone delicately pink and gold. ''You know, we just might suddenly see young Scott evince a tremendous thirst for knowledge. He might begin carrying loads of books home, which I fancy has not been his custom. He could also begin holding after-school consultations with the members of the faculty, even spending hours with Dr. Waring in his office. Gad, I'd like to be in on those sessions! And he could drop a word everywhere that he was busy 'making up his work.' Now we know that isn't physically possible but the students don't. They don't know how low his grades have been. They're young and busy and gullible. They'll swallow it. The point you made that hit Waring right in the belly was that the Seniors might go home telling the tale of how the college had been *bought*. Waring doesn't want that. Not by a pig's tail. But if they fix it that the students will accept Scott's diploma and still believe in Marsden's integrity . . . ."

"And what about the integrity of the faculty?"

"Ah, that we cannot never tell, quoth little Peterkin. But in the words of Shakespeare . . . ."

"Stop," Gavin said sharply. "I can't take another, but I'll give you a real quote, from the immortal bard. 'It smells to heaven.' In other words, the whole thing *stinks*." And he turned on his heel and started to walk rapidly away. After a few paces he came back to where Devereux was still standing beside his car.

"Look, old man, I didn't mean to sound off so violently. It's just that this business has hit me pretty hard."

In a rare gesture Devereux held out his hand. "I couldn't ever get mad at you, Gavin. I respect you too much."

Then he jumped quickly into his car and Gavin started for home. He did a strange thing, however, as he came in sight of Judge McWhorter's house, where he could detect the figure of the old man on the porch. He ducked down a side street and reached home by a circuitous route. He couldn't talk to anybody just now, even the Judge. He must think things through, for his next steps might be precarious indeed. He would tell it all to Cecily tonight, however, for they had long ago decided always to share knowledge with each other even if it might cause pain. This was better than bearing a burden alone and by so doing losing the oneness that had been a special quality of their love.

Dinner that evening somehow was not right. Gavin himself had to force conversation and Cecily seemed to speak also with an effort. Her face was white and drawn as though she were ill.

"Are you all right, darling?" he called down the table to her, anxiously.

"Of course. Just a little tired." He could tell she had difficulty with the smile and it worried him.

Bruce, after his first hunger was appeased, brought the lighter news to the family.

"Say," he began, looking across at Rose, "I heard Abe Williams brought down the house today. I was talking to Pete Mills. He's in the play, Dad, and he said when Abe sang his love song, the whole cast in the wings applauded! He said Abe's voice is always pretty wonderful for a young fellah, but today he simply pulled out all the stops. Isn't that right, Rose?"

"I guess you would say that."

"How about his lines?" Gavin asked eagerly. "Did he do any better with them?"

"Well, yes, a little," Rose said rather grudgingly. Then, "Oh," she burst out, "I don't know which is worse, to play up to him when he's like a fence post or to have him play up to me when he's trying to do a love scene. I wish I could get out of the whole thing!"

"Now, if that isn't like a girl!" Bruce said. "You've been grousing and moaning because Abe played like a wooden Indian and now since he's put some real oomph into it, you don't like that either. You know, Mother,

Pete says he thinks the show's going to be terrific. We haven't had any sort of opera for years, nor a costume play. I think, Rose, you ought to be pretty darned glad you're in it. Pete says you're not bad, either." His praise had brotherly restraint.

"I don't know whether I can bear so much flattery," Rose said with heavy sarcasm, at which Bruce laughed as though all was now right.

"O.K. I'll tell you what he really said after dark when your blushes won't show."

But no one joined Bruce in his witticism and the meal went on quietly with Gavin looking often at Cecily's white face.

"Say, Pop," Ian said, apparently with an effort at last, "I just wondered if I could have the car tonight. After all I've had my license three months now and everything, and I just thought if no one else was planning to use it, maybe . . ."

"Where are you going?" Gavin asked.

"Well, just to the movies but I thought we'd go to the Cameo and from where she lives it's really quite a walk, and gee, it does look sort of better to pick a girl up in a car."

"You don't need it, Bruce, I suppose?" his father asked jestingly.

There was a small wave of laughter for

Bruce's date would be little Phoebe Henderson who lived only a block away.

"I don't want the car tonight, either, so it's all yours, Ian," his father said. "But please drive carefully and promise me one thing, word of honor."

"Name it."

"That you won't go out of town. You're doing very well but you can't become a first-rate driver in three months. I want to be along when you go out to the country. Agreed?"

"Righto and thanks, Pop."

"I'll do the dishes, Mother," Rose said as they all got up.

"All right, dear. And after that are you . . . ?"

"I'm going up to my room to work on the play," she said, with what seemed to Gavin an unnecessary quickness.

He went on up to his small study on the second floor made from what had once been the "sewing-room" during the more affluent days of the house. He found, however, that he could not work. He ended by sitting blankly at his desk while the events of the faculty meeting passed and repassed through his mind. When he remembered Devereux's predictions he put his head in his hands.

Cissie knocked and came in a moment on her way to bed; he heard Rose come up to her room and close the door; then at last, the boys left, calling their good-nights as they went. When all was quiet he went downstairs where Cecily was sitting staring at the wall across from her, a book, untouched, on her knee. He went over to her, put a hand on either arm of her chair and as she raised her head, kissed her.

"Darling," he said, "would you mind coming up now to our own room? I have something I have to talk to you about and I don't want any interruption."

She rose slowly. "I was just about to say that to you," she said.

They went up the broad stairs, hand in hand, as they often did. When they reached their room, Cecily sank down on the chintz-covered chair and Gavin paced back and forth before he spoke. "Cecily," he said at last, "there's something I have to tell you even though I know it will worry you, but I want you to know it all from the beginning. I'm afraid I'm in trouble at college over Lester Scott. You see he's . . . ."

Cecily interrupted him with a hysterical cry. She sprang from the chair and clung to him while his arms enfolding her could feel her trembling.

"What is it?" he said. "Tell me, no matter what. I'm terrified. Are you sick?"

She shook her head. Half laughing, he raised it from his breast. "You're not going to have . . . a baby?"

"No . . . no, but oh Gavin, I only wish it was me! It's Rose. *She's* in trouble with Lester Scott and he utterly refuses to marry her."

Two

LONG AFTER CECILY had finally fallen into a sleep heavy from tears and the grief beyond them, Gavin lay, watching a tiny thread of light that always persisted in entering at the side of the window shade. It came from the electric lantern on a garage on the street behind them. Once when about to make love Gavin had spoken of this querulously.

"I don't like that little nosy bit of light coming in. It's like the Eye of God watching us."

Cecily had laughed. "But dear boy, we're not doing anything *wrong.*"

"Certainly not," he had answered, drawing her closer.

Nothing wrong then, or ever. If they had had to wait for months or a year before their marriage he knew that he could never have touched her beautiful body except with a husband's right. He remembered they had lightly discussed this whole matter between them and were in perfect agreement. That was over twenty years ago and he was aware even then that plenty of his friends did not share his ideas on sex and marriage, or as they were then known, *ideals;* but now in this present day even in conservative old Marsden, its traditions supported by the solid citizens who sent their sons and daughters there to be educated, he realized well enough that the new freedom was at work, had oh, unbelievable, insupportable pain, touched their own child, their darling. Rose.

He lay, watching the Eye of God and wondering if there really were gradations of anguish. There must be. When they waited for a week not knowing whether Ian would lose his leg or not; when they watched with the doctor that awful night when each short breath Bruce had drawn seemed to be his last; when he, Gavin, alone and frenzied had wandered through the hospital corridors, storming heaven with his prayers for Cecily's life and that of the fragile bit of humanity she had borne; even now the remembrance of these crises had power to make him shudder.

Yet there was a difference between them

and the grief and shock now engulfing them. With the former there had been hope, even at the worst there had been the possibility of a cure, a valid reason for prayer. But now in the present case there was no cure possible. They were in the grip of an immutable law of nature. What was there to pray for? Only guidance, Gavin thought. God knows I need that, and perhaps restraint. For his hands clenched and unclenched as though they were gripping the boy who had brought this disaster upon them. That he would *dare* to refuse to marry Rose when he wasn't worthy to touch her shoe! The arrogance, the dastardly, unbelievable selfishness of him! Well, when he got through with him . . . And yet there Gavin stopped with a despairing feeling of certainty. He knew Rose had told her mother the truth about Lester. He would never assume a responsibility; he would never cut short his gay, carefree existence. But suppose pressure could be brought to bear upon him through his father? The thin thread of light seemed suddenly to pierce Gavin's very soul. If, for instance, it were possible to make a *deal*. If the boy's graduation was dependent upon his marriage with Rose? What then?

Gavin suddenly sat up on the side of the

bed, and bowed his head on his hands. What would he do in such a case? He, who had sat in righteous judgment upon his colleagues? I will not face up to that, he thought. Not yet.

It was past three o'clock and he decided to go down to the kitchen and make himself a drink of hot milk with enough rum in it to insure him a few hours' sleep. He went softly out of the room in order not to wake Cecily, and, as softly, along the hall. Outside Rose's room he stopped short for there were sounds within it. Not sobs, rather the long racking breaths which come when the fount of tears is at last dry. He opened the door. "Rose?" he said. There was no answer. "May I come in, dear?"

He walked over to the bed, finding it easily although there was no light, and leaned over her. "Rose," he said again gently.

For answer she threw herself into his arms. "Oh Daddy, you don't hate me, then?"

He sat down on the bed and drew her close. "That," he said, "is about the silliest question I ever heard."

"But I'm so ashamed and so scared. *What am I going to do?*"

"That's what we have to think about. You say Lester does not want to get married?"

"He won't. That's final. He's planning on a year's travel after he graduates and he says no matter how much he l—likes me he will *not* marry me. He offered to take me to the city to a doctor who he knows is good and . . ."

"Oh, my God!" Gavin burst out as his arms tightened about her.

"Well, don't worry. I'm not going to do *that*. I'm afraid. I know a girl who did that and she died. But oh, Daddy, what on earth is to become of me?"

He laid his cheek against hers. "You've heard me speak often of Aunt Het over in Edinburgh. I lived with her, you know, till my uncle thought she was spoiling me and brought me over to this country. No matter what happened Aunt Het would say, *'There's always a way.'* As to Lester, we'll see what will happen when I've talked to him . . ."

"Daddy!" Rose's voice was all but hysterical. "You've got to promise me on your honor that you'll never say a word to him about marriage. I have some pride left. I will never *force* a man to marry me, no matter what happens. That would only compound the shame. You do see that, don't you?"

"Yes," he said slowly, "I guess I do. Maybe his father will influence him, though."

"I doubt it. And there's one more thing I want you to know. I've always been up to this what you and Mother would call a *good girl*. You know. I've had pretty strong feelings about that. I've been so sure of myself. Lester's been hard to handle but I managed it up to that one night. We'd driven out to the reservoir and there was a full moon. Les brought a blanket from the car. It was such a mild night. We sat there watching the light on the water and he seemed *so* terribly in love and I was too. I thought he meant marriage right after graduation, the way he talked."

Her voice was bitter.

"You don't love him now?"

"Not after the way he's acted. But if he would marry me—of his own accord—of course that would be the only way out." She drew a long, despairing sigh.

"Listen," Gavin said. "You made me give you a promise. Now I want you to give me one. On your honor. I want you to put this out of your mind as much as you can, for the present, while your mother and I are doing some thinking. I want you to make yourself laugh, and sing and be gay, as you've always been. You've been pretty edgy lately. Now, be cheerful and pleasant again at home and at college. Never for one moment let even your best friend or any other living soul know there's anything the matter. That would be fatal. If the subject of Lester comes up, just shrug and say you got a little tired of his assurance. Oh, you'll know how to word it. But put on a front. You have exams and the play coming up to fill your thoughts. Will you promise to do this, Rose?" He held out his hand. And she put hers slowly into it.

"I'll try my best. Oh, Daddy, I do feel better since you and Mother know and will still stand by me."

He stooped and kissed her tenderly.

"My dear child, did you ever dream we *wouldn't* stand by you?"

Once out in the hall again he stood for a moment considering. He felt strangely relaxed since his talk with Rose. He gave up the idea of the hot drink and went back to bed.

The next day was Saturday, Cecily's one holiday of the week. Gavin had ordained this long ago and he still carried her tray up to her while the others rose when they pleased and got their own breakfasts. This made a pleasant break in the regular pattern for all of them. This morning Gavin, to his amazement, slept late. When he woke, Cecily was sitting up against her pillow, looking at him.

"Hi, darling," he said. "When I did get to sleep I really overdid it. I was wandering round last night and ended up in Rose's room." He gave her briefly the substance of their talk. "And as soon as I've had breakfast I'm going straight to see Loren Scott. Little as I think of Lester, I agree with Rose that marriage with him would be her only way out."

He brought up Cecily's tray, trying hard to do what he had adjured Rose to do: put up a cheerful front. When he had finished his own breakfast he got in the car and drove to the Scott mansion on the farther edge of town. Almost grimly ostentatious, its gray stone spread amongst the relieving trees and gardens. Gavin's heart was thudding as he rang the bell and then gave his name to the butler. "My errand is urgent," he added.

When he was ushered into Scott's library (where at a glance Gavin guessed the walls of books were for decoration only) the older man rose from his desk and faced his guest pleasantly. He was in his last sixties, bald, corpulent and heavy jowled. His eyes were set a trifle close. His son's good looks had not come from his father.

"Well, Professor, how are you? And what brings you to me this fine morning?" he began.

"A very serious matter," Gavin said. He had decided before that the best method would be direct attack. "My daughter, Rose, is in trouble, your son is responsible, and he so far has refused to marry her. I came to beg you to use your influence to make him do so."

Scott looked surprised but not, to Gavin's horror, too disturbed.

"Well now, Mr. McAllister, I'm sorry of course for your daughter's problem but as to my son's responsibility, neither you nor I could prove that. You know the present times. There may have been others involved."

With one spring Gavin was at his throat. Without any volition of his own he shook, he choked the older man until he saw his face turn scarlet and his eyes bulge with fear. He desisted then at once, the rage still burning within him.

"Take that back," he gritted, "or I'll not

63

be responsible for what I do."

Scott looked at him with malevolence as he breathed heavily and loosened his collar.

"McAllister," he said at last, "I will tell no one of this unwarranted attack upon my person or the reason for it, for I know you are in great mental stress. But I will not *forget* it! As to my influencing my son to marry your daughter I would even urge him against it. He is young, handsome, wealthy with his life before him. I expect to send him to Europe after graduation to make the *Grand Tour,* as it used to be called. He certainly at this point is not going to be saddled with a wife and a child. As to any financial consideration, that is different. I withdraw my earlier words," he added as an afterthought, then stopped, looking at Gavin who stood, stunned, before him. "I will meet any figure you name," he said.

Gavin gave him one terrible look, and rushed from the room, and the house. He got into his car and drove as fast as he dared until he reached Judge McWhorter's yellow brick. He found the Judge in his own library lined with the well-read books of the years.

"Well, Gavin!" he said delightedly, "this is a pleasant . . ."

"Judge, I've just nearly killed a man."

"And what else is new?" the Judge returned cheerfully. "Gavin, I wish you wouldn't run yourself ragged every spring over those students of yours. They ain't worth it. You look like the devil."

"Judge, I mean it. I honestly came within an ace of choking a man. It's shaken me! I never dreamed I could be guilty of such a . . ."

"Who were you mixin' it with, for God's sake?" The Judge was still calmly curious.

"Loren Scott."

"Well," the Judge considered, "if you'd done him in I doubt if I'd have been at the funeral. But I'd have *approved* of it. I never liked the man. What's itchin' you at Scott?"

"He made a foul remark about Rose and I sprang at him."

At once all levity left the Judge's countenance. His eyes were gimlets as they pierced Gavin.

"Rose?" he repeated. "You'd better tell me everything as fast as you can."

"That's what I came to do." He told it all then in its stark and wretched simplicity.

The Judge leaned his head above his desk and spread both hands before his face. There was silence except for now and then small muffled words from behind the fingers as the

65

tears seeped through them.

"Not little Rosie! Not little Rosie!" he kept whispering.

At last Gavin said, "There are so few courses we have to choose from. Thank God Rose herself eliminated the worst, the most dangerous one. But, there are left only two as I can see it . . ."

"Be quiet!" the Judge said. "I've got to think." So silence settled again. Indeed Gavin began to feel it was never to be broken, when the Judge slowly raised his head, wiped his eyes and spoke.

"She must marry. This must be arranged. Even if the marriage is later dissolved, this I'm sure will be the best in the long run. Now, I will tell you something. I sat on the bench for thirty years, and I studied the faces of every man or woman on trial. I watched them. And many a time my charge to the jury or the sentence I pronounced was determined by what I'd read in their countenances. One special time I remember. I don't recall clearly the details of the case. It was long ago. The man on trial I had a feeling was being framed by his brother-in-law. There was money involved, and there entered into it the charge that he had been cruel to his wife. This he denied vehemently but the evidence was ticklish. The wife had been sick. When she finally came into the courtroom I watched the husband. And as he saw her, there passed over his face something like *a light*. It's hard to describe but I knew instantly that he loved her. I gave my charge with that knowledge in mind. Now, Gavin, what I'm getting at is this. In your classrooms, have you ever seen a boy —they're men now—look at Rose as if he loved her? I don't mean that damned Scott boy, I mean another. Did you ever see this?"

Gavin sat, staring at him, a strange, forgotten remembrance returning.

"Did you?" the Judge pressed, his gimlet eyes growing sharper.

"I never saw anything that would help our problem in the least."

"That's not what I asked you. Did you ever see a boy look at Rose when he thought no one saw him, with the light of love on his face? Did you?"

"Well," Gavin hesitated, "I had forgotten until you asked, but once while I was monitoring an exam I did see a certain expression on a boy's face. But Judge, as I'm trying to tell you, this can't lead anywhere. This boy is impossible."

"He's not decent? He's not good?"

"Oh, yes. Both. But it happens Rose doesn't like him. She can't *stand* him."

"Fine," said the Judge. "Couldn't be better. That's the way lots of women begin to be attracted. Now Gavin, there's no time for delay. You have one thing to work on. Start at once. It may not come to anything, but it's worth a trial. If you can find a decent boy who will accept the situation and keep his mouth shut, then we'll let the Lord attend to the future. It's the present we have to manipulate."

"But . . . but Rose?" Gavin's voice broke on the words.

The Judge's eyes filled up again. "I know," he said, "I know. She will have to drain the bitter cup now, but she has all her life ahead of her, and she must have the protection of a man's name for herself and the child."

"She could go away and then give up . . . the child?"

The Judge shook his head. "I know a lot about that procedure. There are two strong reasons against it. It would always haunt her. And it would somehow become known. I've watched that happen. Asses' ears, you know. But if a girl marries, and has a baby several months too soon, people lift their eyebrows but they accept it and forget it. That's the difference."

Gavin got up to go, drawing a long, heavy sigh. "Do hearts break, Judge?"

"No," the older man said, "they crack. Then after time has passed, they mend. I ought to know. Go ahead, Gavin. You're a strong man. Keep me posted, will you? I'll go on thinking about this. I may even go so far as to pray a little. *That* ought to give you an idea how deeply I feel."

He waved his farewell and Gavin left. As he drove home he smiled in spite of himself. The Judge in his emotional stress had forgotten all about his grammarian's revolt. He had spoken as he might have done on the bench. But his advice? How could he possibly take it?

He told Cecily quietly in the kitchen the substance of Loren Scott's refusal. He did not mention his remark concerning Rose nor his own reaction. He would tell that later. "Keep up, darling," he said. "It's most important that we do."

"Bob has been calling you," she told him. "He wanted you to get in touch with him at once when you came in."

Gavin went wearily to the telephone. Bob

St. Clair was the closest friend he had among his contemporaries, a trial lawyer, and a bachelor who had made their home a sort of haven. A call from him was always welcome except now, when his own heart was so heavy.

"Hi, Bob," he said when there was an answering voice, "what's on your mind?"

"It's Billy King. He's on a real rampage this time, stoned to the teeth. I happened by and heard the ruckus and went in. He's calling for you. Could you come? I hate to see the police get hold of him. I just came out to phone you. Can you make it?"

Gavin drew a quick breath. "As soon as I grab a sandwich," he said. "Just stay with him till I get there."

"O.K. Bring an extra one along. From the look of things he hasn't had much to eat. I'll get right back."

Gavin told Cecily briefly and she set to work at once packing a basket of eatables. "Poor old soul!" she said. "But poor *you*, to have this on top of everything else today."

"Where is everybody?"

"Oh, the boys are out on their own affairs. Rose is still sound asleep. I suppose she hasn't slept much lately. You haven't thought of . . . anything?"

70

"There hasn't been much time yet. We'll talk tonight. Get some rest this afternoon, darling, if you can."

It was something of a mystery to Gavin, himself, just how he had become general custodian of Billy King. He had met the man soon after his own coming to Marsden. Tall, seedy as to clothes, and yet with a touch of bygone dignity in features and bearing, Billy had been walking with apparent care and frequent deviation from the straight line one day toward Gavin. When he came up to him he stopped.

"Professor McAllister, I presume?"

"Correct, Mr. Stanley," Gavin grinned, his reply automatic.

The effect upon the man before him had been startling. He stared incredulously and then, throwing back his head to the imminent peril of his attempt to maintain the perpendicular, he gave way to great chuckling laughs. "My mirth," he said when he could speak, while Gavin steadied him, "is caused by the fact that you're the first person I've found in this God-damned town who has a sense of humor. Or maybe it's just that nobody credits *me* with having one. At any rate I thank you, sir, for both, and I hope we meet again. My name is William King."

71

But when he had attempted to go on Gavin felt he must continue his steadying arm. So it came about that he went along down a side street and into a narrow entrance behind a hardware store to the small apartment where Billy lived.

"Not just my idea of a gentleman's residence, but come in, sir," he had said then.

Gavin had managed to get him safely inside and seated on a chair before he left. He had in the short time glimpsed the untidy room furnished with cheap odds and ends, the dust, the unwashed dishes on the table, but also a long shelf of books and two pictures which he was sure were good ones. William King, then, was evidently a man with a past. Gavin had promised to come back again when as his host put it, "he was feeling stronger." And over the years, faithful to that promise, he had dropped in when he could, to talk with Billy when he was reasonably sober, for Plato was on the shelf, and Browning, Amiel's *Journal* and Shakespeare and the *Oxford Book of Enqlish Verse,* among others. And he calmed him down with severity if necessary when Billy was delirious from drink. While the latter, sensing a warm heart as well as a strong will in his new friend, clung to him with an almost desperate affection.

Today as Gavin drove toward the alley entrance his brain felt numb as though, like a child, he had watched a kaleidoscope, none of its events being real. When Bob came to the door with Billy's drunken shouts behind him he peered curiously at his friend.

"What's wrong, Gavin? You look used up."

"Oh, this is a tough time at college. End of the year, you know. Exams in the offing. All that."

"Well, gad, I hope this isn't the last straw for you. You're the only one who can always quiet him and this is the worst he's ever been to my knowledge, so I felt I had to send for you. Good luck. Give me a ring from the hardware store if you need me. I'll be in my office."

Gavin went in. The room was a shambles for Billy had evidently been throwing the furniture about. He sat on a chair now shaking and shouting. Gavin caught his hands hard in his own for a minute. "Shut up, Billy," he said firmly. "Now just quiet down. I've brought you something to eat."

He poured the hot coffee then from the Thermos bottle and held it while Billy slowly drank. He fed him a sandwich, some sponge cake and poured some coffee. The man was quiet now, though still trembling.

"What's wrong, Billy?"

"I'm scared."

"Scared of what?"

"Hell," Billy uttered in a hoarse whisper.

"When did this hit you?"

"Last night. Mac, it was awful. I saw the flames. That's where I'll go. Burning fire forever." He began to shake again.

Gavin's voice was angry. "Billy, you're an intelligent person when you're sober. How can you believe a thing like that?"

"Don't you believe in . . . h-*hell?*"

"Certainly not. Not the kind you're talking about. I think that's an insult to the Almighty."

Billy drew a shuddering breath. "It never hit me before till last night. Then I saw the fire and I thought of all eternity in it and I just about went crazy. You're *s-sure,* Mac?"

"I'm not sure of many things, Billy, but I'm perfectly sure of this."

The shaking gradually stopped. His voice was wistful. "I don't suppose I could expect anyway to get to heaven. Wherever that is," he said.

"Might be right around us, for all we

know," Gavin replied absently, and then added, looking off over the old man's head:

"O world invisible we view thee,
O world intangible we touch thee . . ."

The drunken man suddenly sat up straighter. A light of recognition came into his watery red eyes.

"F-Francis T-Thompson," he stammered triumphantly.

"Right. And a beautiful poem it is. Now, can you get yourself into the bathroom and wash up? You need it. Cecily sent enough food for you for tomorrow and I'll put it in the icebox and then help you to bed."

When Billy was at last settled there, Gavin put a cool cloth on his head and drew the covers up as though he were a child. And like a child Billy pressed his friend's hand and fell instantly to sleep.

Gavin straightened up the furniture in the other room a little and then went out to his car. "All I needed to complete my day," he muttered to himself, "was to pull Billy out of hellfire."

As he drove home he kept considering the life of the man he had just left, partly as an anodyne to stave off the torturing thoughts out of which he and Cecily must make a decision that night if possible. Right now his weary mind refused to contemplate its urgency. So, he thought of Billy. In bits and pieces over the years he had gathered the story. Orphaned during his Senior year in college, Billy had been left with a small patrimony, a taste for literature and art and an apparently weak will. He had betaken himself at once to Paris, where he studied painting, lived on the Left Bank, drank absinthe and indulged in other and expensive excesses. In spite of praise from his teacher Billy had grown less willing to work. Endless discussions of art in the abstract at cafés took the place of its actual practice. By the time he was thirty he had accomplished little and to his horror had spent all his money.

He had one relative, Aunt Bessie, who lived in a modestly comfortable apartment in New York with four cats. She had inherited the family taste for art and had herself spent a year or two in Paris in her girlhood, "studying," as she always put it. Now, except for her beloved felines, she was lonely; Billy arrived as a godsend, and *remained*. With him she had someone with whom she could discuss Paris, and painting, and literature, but greatest boon of all, he provided her now with an *escort*. Together they went to the theater, concerts and all the art shows, and together also, unfortunately, they drank many nightcaps as they discussed what they had seen and heard.

Along the way Billy had found various jobs, but lost each after some months, due to his inability to get up in the morning and get to work on time. So he sank at last with Aunt Bessie into a soft dilettantism which suited them both.

Aunt Bessie died at seventy, leaving her current cats generously provided for, the rest of her estate to the Society for the Prevention of Cruelty to Animals except for a trust fund for Billy. The income, about one hundred and fifty dollars a month, was to be paid during his lifetime, at the end of which the *corpus* would go also to the S.P.C.A. Her furnishings, which the second-hand dealer declared were worth little, were also left to Billy and provided him at least with enough cash to leave the city where he felt he could no longer live. Expressing a box of books and the two best paintings, he had set out with two suitcases for Marsden which was to him then only a name he had heard Aunt Bessie mention often in connection with a school friend long since dead. He had liked the sound of it and had come, since one place now was as good as another. A man at the hotel knew of the apartment behind the hardware store and Billy had taken it at once. It was solidly built, freshly painted, adequate for his needs, and low in rent. Moreover he liked the location. He would have quiet and the little alley-like entrance would have advantages if he received nocturnal callers. He frequently referred to himself bitterly as "Aunt Bessie's Tom Cat," especially when his monthly stipend ran low. But Gavin kept reminding him that he would have enough to live on if his liquor bills were not so enormous. Since he had been able to secure Pernod (even while lamenting it was not absinthe) he subsisted largely upon it, and it was not cheap.

"I wonder, Mac," he had said one day, "whether you know that Pernod is an aphrodisiac?"

"I believe I've heard so," Gavin answered.

Billy had looked his friend over critically. "But you don't need it, I would surmise?"

"I think not."

"No," Billy went on, "with your virility and your beautiful wife . . ."

"That's enough," Gavin cut in sharply. "We will not discuss this further."

"O.K. Just remember though, Mac, that you should have compassion on a man who does not have your blessings."

Compassion! Gavin was thinking to himself now, as his own house came into view. That was the only attitude that could be taken toward Billy. What a wasted life! Where in the whole scheme of things could it ever be said to have any significance?

At the moment, though, it had served a purpose. Gavin's concentration upon Billy had kept in abeyance the other thoughts which would soon rise to smite him. As he entered the house everything, to his relief, seemed normal. Rose was talking on the telephone, the boys evidently not back yet, and the sweet smell of baking pie was rising from the kitchen. He went through to speak to Cecily.

"A boy's been calling Rose up," she said.

"Not Lester?" he asked quickly.

"Oh, no. I didn't recognize his voice. Rose is talking to him now. How's Billy?"

"Left him asleep. He'll be all right by tomorrow."

"Bob called up to know how you got on. He said he would drop by tonight."

"I think I'll beg off from that," Gavin said. "We must be alone and talk things

79

over. I'll give Bob a ring if I can think of a good excuse. Could you have a headache?"

"I not only could but do," she answered. "Even though I had a nap."

"Poor darling," he said softly, for they heard Rose coming.

"Hi," she said in her usual voice. "I certainly made up arrears in sleep today. Thanks to you both," she added under her breath. "I'm going out tonight."

"With whom and to what?" Gavin asked as he nibbled a piece of sugared pie crust which Cecily always baked because he liked it.

"Oh, with Dave Jordan. He's not very exciting but he's a nice guy. A few of the boys just suddenly got the idea of a hamburger picnic out at Beecham's Woods tonight. They're going to bring the meat and the beer and cokes. We girls are to take the rolls."

"You certainly get off easily," Cecily said. "When I think of our old Vermont picnics when I was in my teens! We girls took sandwiches and every conceivable kind of cake and the boys brought a freezer of ice cream. Why has cake gone out of style, Rose?"

"I haven't noticed that it has in this

family," Gavin remarked.

"I mean in general amongst the young people."

"Oh," said Rose "the girls won't eat it for fear it makes them fat and the boys can't eat it with beer, so that rules out the cake. Well, I'd better get on downtown and get my rolls. I'm going to get good ones at the bakery. Anything I can do for you, Mother?"

"No thanks, dear. I think I'm all set."

When she was gone, Cecily looked at Gavin. "You ought to get a bit of rest before dinner. Do go up and lie down."

"I believe I will if I can't do anything for you here. I'll give Bob a ring, for I don't want to talk to anyone tonight but you."

When he was in the bedroom he took off his coat, kicked off his shoes and stretched out, exhausted. His eyes, however, refused to stay closed. His glance took in the familiar details: the soft florals of the wallpaper with the chintz chair matching, Cecily's dresser with the Cupid lamps he had given her one Christmas and the neat array of her toilet articles, his own chest with Cecily's wedding picture upon it and the photographs of the family made a few years ago. The curtains moved softly like white clouds in the breeze and all was as usual, with memories of love experienced, the intimate conversations about children, work and friends which take place between a man and woman alone at night, and weaving through all, laughter, much laughter. All this the room had always held. But now there was a beclouding, a darkness that would not lift.

The strange question which he had tried to parry that morning had been answered unequivocally in his own mind. He had once many months ago seen on a boy's face the very light the Judge had described. It had been for a moment there and then gone, and Gavin had never thought of it again. Until today. The boy whose countenance had borne this sudden look of love had been Abe Williams. Gavin at the back of the classroom had followed the glance and seen Rose with her lovely head raised, thinking. He had half smiled at the time, his father's heart gloating over his child's beauty. Then all was as before and the instant gone like a breath. But now that it had been strangely recalled from memory's unpredictable storehouse, what was he to do with it? What *could* he do with it?

Abe Williams. Tall, shy, awkward, with clothes neat and clean but shabby. "He obnoxes me," Rose had said once bitterly in the ridiculous slang of the day. *Honest Abe, the butt of the girls' jokes.*

But there was also the boy he himself knew, the Abe with the sensitive nature, the brilliant mind, and the fine, mature taste in literature. The one who looked you straight in the eye. This was the man, for of course he *was* a man now, with the solid qualities of the old country behind him, along with his special racial inheritance. And, for whatever it mattered, without, apparently, a penny to his name. Even considering the Judge's vast experience and profound wisdom, what could possibly be done about Abe even though he loved Rose? And could it have been only last night that here in this room he had said to Cecily, "I'm in trouble at college over Lester Scott," and she had poured out the greater, the agonizing trouble which had driven the first problem out of his mind all this day? It all seemed to him to have happened years ago, so old can suffering become within the hours. He lay, quietly sorting out the facts he would present to Cecily that night, feeling about in his benumbed brain for new ones; then as he finally heard young voices downstairs he knew it must be dinnertime.

During the meal all on the surface was

cheerfully normal. Bruce was in particularly fine spirits.

"Well, guess what?" he said to Rose. "Phoebe and I are going to the hamburger fry tonight."

"How come?"

"Just comes, that's all. I was with some of the fellahs while they were planning it and they said why not bring my date and join the spree. Oh, Pop, I forgot about the car. Are you wanting it tonight?"

"Not a bit. It's all yours . . . and Phoebe's," he added. "She's a very attractive little girl, Bruce."

"Thanks," he said, blushing to the roots of his hair. "Say, Mom, this pie's the greatest! Any chance for me to have that last piece?"

"Now, see here, swinelet . . ." Ian began.

Cecily smiled at them. "By the oddest coincidence I made two. Bring in the other one, will you, Rose?"

At last that night the house was quiet, the young folks departed and little Cissie in bed. Gavin put out the downstairs lights. "This will fool any would-be callers into thinking we're out. I'll come down later on and turn them on for the children's return."

They undressed, then lay, hands clasped

but awake, oh most terribly awake, upon the bed. Gavin told Cecily then all that the Judge had said, and then very slowly, his memory's recall.

"Oh, no," Cecily gasped. "Oh, Gavin, even if the boy were willing, we couldn't do *that* to Rose. There will be some other way. There *must* be."

"That brings me to the one constructive thought I've had. When I was talking to Rose last night I remembered how Aunt Het always used to say: *there's always a way.* I wondered if we could send Rose over to Edinburgh to her . . ."

Cecily sat up in bed in her eagerness.

"But Gavin, *of course.* Why didn't we think of that right away. That would be the . . ."

"But wait, darling. It's not so easy. Aunt Het is in her late seventies. We couldn't possibly put on her all the responsibility that will come. Don't you see? From her last letter she sounded well and active enough, but this would be by far too much for her, unless . . ."

"Unless what?"

"Unless Rose went with a husband to care for her and assume the burden. In that case I think this would be an almost unbelievably good solution for the whole situation, but it brings us right back to the matter of marriage.''

Cecily sank against the pillow. "I see that," she said brokenly. "But even if this boy were willing to . . . marry her, she would never agree.''

Gavin's voice sounded harsh for him. "Tragically enough, Rose has put herself into a position where she will have to do what we decide is best for her whether she likes it or not.''

"I've been thinking all day of course, too. There must be some place here in this country at a distance where we could send her and arrange for her care at the last and have her give up the child . . . surely that would be the best way.''

"I don't think so," Gavin said. "Knowing Rose's nature that might always leave a scar. And as the Judge says, it would be like the old story of the asses' ears, the truth would come out. *Someone* would discover it and the news would get back here, as sure as anything. No, I feel if it can possibly be arranged that marriage is best for her. But we are simply hedged about with *ifs*.''

"You think this Abe Williams is in love with her?''

"I have an idea he is. Aside from what I've told you, I remember when I was helping him with his play lines one day he couldn't name Rose without stammering and blushing. 'R-R-Rose is disgusted with me,' he said. I didn't pay any attention to it at the time, but it's another straw in the wind."

"You think he's a *nice* boy?" she quavered.

"Do you suppose for a moment I would be considering this plan if I didn't? I would many times rather see her marry Abe than Lester Scott. He's a born student, too. The kind that ought to go on with his studies."

They lay for a time in wretched silence. Then Gavin spoke.

"One great trouble is that the boy stands to lose so much. We would have to make it clear to them both that this, if it should happen, is not a life sentence for Rose. I don't ever like the idea of divorce, but after a time—a year, two years, whatever—if Rose was miserable in the marriage she would have to have the chance to be free. And what of him? In love with her. *With her beauty!* Oh, that would be cruel. If only there was an incentive, some inducement in addition to Rose herself we could offer him. If there could be . . ."

Gavin's strong frame seemed to stiffen as he grasped his wife's hand until it hurt her. The thin little light, the Eye of God, as he had playfully called it, seemed now again to pierce his very soul. He shuddered under it.

"What is it, Gavin?" she asked anxiously.

He sat up on the edge of the bed and reached for his slippers and dressing gown.

"I'm sorry, darling. Just all at once I feel I've got to get some air. I'll go down to the garden for a few minutes if you don't mind. It's been a heavy day," he added.

"I know. And you've had the hardest part of it. Go on, dear. The garden always helps you."

He went through the darkened house, feeling his way, dreading light as though it were an unbearable weapon. He went out the kitchen door. On the back steps he sank down as though without strength to go further. He sat at first staring into the spring darkness, tense, hands clenched.

"I won't! I can't! It's not fair! That's the end of it," he burst out vehemently.

Then as the soft air filled with new, first-blooming life encompassed him as the moments passed, he slowly, slowly dropped his head on his hands. He spoke no more but great, deep breaths shook him.

It was nearly an hour before Cecily came down and sat beside him. "I couldn't bear for you to be here so long alone. Have . . . have you thought of anything else?"

"Yes, I have," Gavin said, and his voice sounded to him surprisingly firm. "Yes, I have. When I go now to talk to the boy, as I must do soon, I have decided upon an incentive, a real inducement which I can offer him. It just might make all the difference."

For a long minute there was silence, but their thoughts had always been curiously open to each other. Suddenly Cecily drew his head down upon her shoulder as though he were a child. She smoothed his hair. She kissed his forehead and he felt a tear fall upon his cheek.

"Oh, my dearest, I love you so," she said. "I think I know what you intend to do."

Three

So SPEEDILY DO new ideas, whether pleasant, bizarre, or even agonizing, settle themselves in the mind as though they belonged there by right of time and acceptance, that the thought which had come to Gavin the night before seemed to him now as he woke on Sunday morning to be old, invariant, immutable. Cecily had been correct in her surmise. As she had caressed him, broken and spent after his wrestling with the Angel, she had spoken gently, and without remonstrance, to his plan. She knew by long experience the iron quality of his will. She knew also, even as he, that eventually love "carries a burden which is no burden." There was one concrete thing which Gavin had to offer young Williams if he should agree to his strange part in the salvation of Rose. This was the money, accumulated with sacrificial care over the years for the financing of his own study for the Doctorate. It could be used now for another degree.

It was a bright Sunday, sweet-scented with bloom, quiet as always for this street had little traffic even on weekdays, the air softly punctuated by distant bells on the various churches. There was a good deal of chat about the cookout of the night before, Bruce enthusiastically giving most of the details since it was his first time with this older group. "We had a blast, all right," he kept repeating.

"And Mother, guess what?" Rose said suddenly. "Phoebe brought a big devil's food cake just because Bruce likes it and you should have seen everybody fall upon it. The coke-drinkers, that is. The girls threw caution to the winds, and the boys! Well, there wasn't a crumb left. Maybe we'll be getting back to Vermont picnic style yet. Did Phoebe bake it herself, Bruce?"

"Of course," he said, coloring up as he always did when Phoebe's name was mentioned, "She's a wonderful cook. But, you know, I think they impose on her. She has to get dinner nearly every night. Her mother's out afternoons to meetings or to play bridge or something. She's *never* home when the children get there. You're always here, Mother, well, *almost* always, and I must say I like it that way."

"I think, dear," Cecily said gently, "that is one of the nicest compliments I've ever had."

"The Hendersons are just so different from us," Bruce added.

"In what other respects?" Gavin asked.

"Well for instance at the table. I've only been asked there once to dinner, as I guess you know. But it was as stiff as a funeral. Honestly, they act as if they're *afraid* of their father, and their mother too. When Phoebe's over here she says it seems like a different world, the way we all laugh and kid each other. I *pity* her," he ended vehemently.

Cecily spoke at once. "I'll invite her over one night this week to dinner. I don't know Mrs. Henderson well but I'll call her to make it entirely proper. And now, we'd better clear the table and then," she laughed, "get ready, as Doctor Stevens puts it, for the 'offices of the day.' "

"I don't believe I'll go to church this morning," Gavin told her quietly in the kitchen, "but I'll drive you there and pick you up."

"I'd rather walk, really. It's not far and it will do me good. Clear my mind a little. Oh,

Gavin, my dear boy, I wish I could tell you how I feel for you!"

"You never need to," he said. "I know anyway."

The matter of church-going, like many other conservative aspects of Marsden, was well established. While Gavin's personal beliefs were well on the liberal side, his early upbringing and that of Cecily had made it natural for them to conform to town tradition. Indeed Gavin had been approached several times by Dr. Stevens, the minister, with an invitation to become a church officer. This he had steadily declined. Once the good Doctor, who while becomingly orthodox had a sense of humor, had looked quizzically at his parishioner. "I wonder what your religion really is, Gavin," he said.

Gavin only smiled. "It's the religion of all Sensible Men."

"And what is that?"

"Sensible Men don't say," he replied with a chuckle.

But while he had the innate Scottish reticence as far as discussing his inner beliefs was concerned, many of them were deep seated. For example, just as he felt the gold-domed courthouse stood for law and order and justice, so he considered the great stone church with its heaven-pointing finger to be the symbol of man's search for something higher than himself and therefore to be respected and supported.

The boys still attended service with little remonstrance (though not sitting with the family), for a number of college students were always there, gaining thus, by an unobtrusive monitor system, exemption from chapel.

In the quiet of the garden sunshine, after the rest of the household had left, Gavin paced slowly back and forth. " 'If 'twere done when 'tis done,' " he quoted to himself, " 'then 'twere well it were done quickly.' " He would drive out to see Abe Williams that very day, or rather that night. What he had to say would be easier for both of them under cover of darkness.

He began practicing what he would say, more carefully than he had ever worked upon a professional address: the approach; the central and terrible fact; the possibility of Abe's interest, of his own involvement; then the *inducement*. Over and over Gavin worded and re-worded his sentences, draining every vocabulary resource he knew, that the truth, the desperate question, the suggestion of an ultimate solution might somehow not frighten the boy into an abject silence. The matter of entrusting Abe with a secret by its nature so essentially inviolate, did not, strangely enough, worry him. He heard the boy again reading:

"And thou—what needest with thy tribe's
  black tents
Who hast the red pavilion of my heart?"

It was a man capable of mature feeling who had spoken those lines. Whether he agreed or not, he would never break trust, Gavin felt sure.

Before the rest of the family returned he decided to make the phone call and leave a message if necessary. He couldn't very well explain to his young people why he was calling Abe, if they should overhear. Luckily it was the boy himself who answered.

"Oh, Abe? This is Mr. McAllister."

"Why, hello, Professor." His tone held pleased surprise.

"I have a few things I'd like to talk over with you, Abe. If I pick you up tonight, would you be free to take a drive with me?"

"Why yes. Why certainly. Of course," Abe stammered.

"About eight then. And can you direct me how to get to your house? I don't believe I know."

When the conversation was over, Gavin felt his hand tremble as he replaced the phone in its cradle. "I've got to get hold of myself better than this," he muttered. "I can't go to pieces when I talk to the boy."

At the dinner table he looked at his sons. "I hope neither of you was expecting to use the car tonight, for I need it myself. I have to see a man," he added.

"I'm going over to Jack Hart's. He's got a lot of new records. Pretty solid rock, I guess," Ian said.

"I wasn't counting on the car, Dad," Bruce followed up. "I'm just going . . . I mean I won't need the car."

Everyone laughed, for all knew Phoebe Henderson's proximity.

"How about you, Rose?" Gavin asked casually. "Are you going out?"

"Oh, I don't know. Ned Parks has a new electric guitar and he asked a few of us in. Dave Jordan plays pretty well, too, on his. He may drop by for me."

"That sounds like fun," Gavin said.

"But nobody, I repeat, nobody," Cecily announced, "has inquired what Cissie and I are doing this evening!'' Her lovely face was bright, by what effort of will Gavin alone knew.

''As Cissie and I were coming down the church steps,'' she went on, ''we met Mrs. Wilson and her little granddaughter. We stopped to chat and she invited us—just Cissie and me, please note—over for a five o'clock supper. The girls are to play croquet while she and I look at the gardens. Isn't that nice?''

''Delightful,'' Gavin said. ''I'd like to be along for the garden part. Home has promised me some bulbs later when he divides his. Magnificent tulips they have. When do you want to be picked up, Cecily?''

''Oh, I imagine about seven. We shouldn't stay more than two hours.''

''All right. I'll be there. And I think the rest of us can rustle up some supper for ourselves without any trouble.''

By seven-thirty all had gone as planned. The older young folk were upstairs getting dressed for the evening, with Cissie telling the news of her visit with great animation from room to room. Gavin called his good-bye from the hall, then kissed Cecily tenderly at the door. Her eyes brimmed over as she gave him her blessing. He got in the car and drove slowly through the town, past the college and on out the country road Abe had designated. It was quiet except for a faint peeping chorus of young frogs rising from a marshy meadow. As his eyes grew accustomed to the early dusk Gavin watched intently the fields on either side and the brooding woods beyond them. This was what Abe saw every day on his walk to and from college. What might his thoughts be as he made this journey? Were they ever of Rose? Were they fixed upon what his future would hold? Gavin had, of course, no idea, but as he tried to imagine the inner workings of the boy's mind he drove more and more slowly and at the crossroads he stopped the car and sat leaning upon the wheel. *I can't go on with this,* he told himself. *It's utterly impossible. It's fantastic. We've got to think of another way.*

Then as he was about to turn the car, he saw the face of the Judge, tear-streaked, saddened but implacable in its wisdom. Gavin took the left fork as Abe had indicated and before long drew up before the Williams' home. It was a small old farmhouse but evidently kept in good repair. Everything around it was neat; the grass cut, the fence whitewashed; the orchard at the side cared for. He did not have to go in; to his relief Abe was waiting for him and came out at once to the car.

"Hello, Professor," he said as he got in. "Have you got some more ideas for me? I could use a few, though I think I'm really a little better than I was, thanks to you."

Gavin didn't answer as he drove on down the road and stopped at the edge of the woods. Abe looked at him keenly. "Is anything wrong?" he asked.

All at once Gavin's carefully prepared *approach* went out the window. His voice shook on the words but they seemed to burst from him.

"Yes, there is. It's Rose. She's in trouble. I guess you know what I mean."

"Oh, my God!" the boy said under his breath. Then he hissed the word, *"Scott?"*

"Yes. But he won't marry her."

"I could kill him with my own hands. Oh, he's a dirty dog."

"Abe," Gavin said quietly, "by any chance are you in love with Rose?"

For what seemed an eternity the boy did not answer. Then he said slowly, "For a good while now."

"What she needs is the protection of a good man's name for herself and her . . ."

Abe broke in almost with violence. "But Mr. McAllister, Rose wouldn't *look* at me, she's so far above me. I really think she finds me sort of disgusting. And the minute I'm with her I get scared. I can't talk to her. I'm not much good with any girls but I'm worst of all with Rose because I'm . . . well, because of the way I feel about her. Can't you see I couldn't possibly do anything for her no matter how much I might want to? And I'm so damned poor, too," he added.

"Let's forget about that for a while," Gavin spoke gently. "This is the hardest problem I've ever had to solve, Abe. And it's not solved yet by a good deal. I have thought of one or two possibilities, however. The first was you, and I had to begin with you."

"What made you ever think I—loved Rose?"

"I saw you look at her once when you thought no one was noticing. Oh, a couple of little things. Enough to make me take the chance. Now the other thing I've thought of is this. I grew up till my teens in Scotland. An aunt took me in when my parents died. She still lives in Edinburgh. She's old and alone now, and I imagine of course lonely. If Rose, *with a husband,* could go over there for say a year or eighteen months nobody

100

here would know what happened."

"But I'm telling you, Mr. McAllister . . ."

"Wait till you hear it all, Abe. The trouble is it seems unfair to you even to mention the whole of my plan for fear it won't work."

"Well, I can tell you right now that it won't."

"But you, yourself, would be willing?"

"Of course," he said very low. "What do you suppose? But she can't stand me and I've no money at all."

"I have," Gavin said. "I have some savings and nothing important to do with it compared to helping Rose. I thought in the event you two could marry and go over to stay at my aunt's I could finance you while you got your Master's degree at the University of Edinburgh. I think you could get a delay from the draftboard for that."

He was watching the boy and he saw his face turn white.

"My Master's!" he whispered.

"In English. That's your best subject. Have you ever thought of teaching?"

"Ever since I've known you," Abe said simply.

"I can tell by your face what this would mean to you. You're a born student and a degree from Edinburgh would give you real prestige over here whenever you would be through with your service. But Abe, I have to remind you again, that none of this may happen."

"You don't need to remind me," Abe said with a sad bitterness in his voice, "but I thank you anyway. I'll always remember that you . . . that you thought of this. That you thought of me."

"And I must ask you on your honor never to breathe a word of this conversation."

"You can certainly trust me on that."

Then for a little while there was silence except for soft night sounds from the woods and the meadow. When Gavin finally spoke it seemed an unrelated question.

"Does your family have a car, Abe?"

"No, we don't now. You see we needed a tractor terribly, so we sold the car and one way and another we managed to get the tractor. It's made a big difference with the farm work."

"Then," Gavin went on thoughtfully, "you couldn't very well ask a girl for a date."

"A *date?*" Abe repeated, the bitterness still in his tone. "What girl would go out with me? But the car would be the easiest part. My uncle lives with us. He's got a nice enough one that he uses to drive to work every day. He's lent it to me for night rehearsals.''

"Well, that's fine. Now Abe, I want you to call Rose up and invite her to go to the movies. You can talk to her about the play on the way there and back. There must be a few little things still to be ironed out, I imagine.''

"Oh, there are.''

"This will give you a good chance to discuss them. I think it will do you both good, give you more confidence in your parts, for you never talk together except on the stage, do you?''

"Never.''

"Well, then, please do as I ask you.''

"She won't . . . Mr. McAllister, I'd do anything for you, but believe me, this won't work.''

"Try it,'' Gavin said, as he turned the car. "As a favor to me, *try it.*''

On the way home his feelings were mixed. Overall perhaps was a small hope, a minuscule sense of triumph that the first great question had been answered in the affirmative. But beyond the boy was Rose herself. He felt an upsurging of pity for her, not just for her condition, but that, unknown to her, and certainly in opposition to her heart, to her most delicate and intimate feelings, there was being set in motion a plan from which perhaps she could not escape. He groaned. *I don't like the idea of playing God,* he thought. *This is a terrible, an awful responsibility.* As the Judge had decreed, he was manipulating events, but also two young lives, and oh, who could tell the outcome of that?

The next morning for the first time in his ten years of professorship at Marsden, Gavin entered his classroom with reluctance. In the first place, in point of time, his immediate view of the spot where the new library would eventually stand brought a feeling of misery. He saw at once as he went up to his desk that no notice of a faculty meeting was upon it. Waring, evidently then, was thinking the matter over. In the next place as he stood looking over the empty chairs he realized with various pangs that in the Senior English period he would see Rose's lovely face with the strained, fearful look in her eyes, raised to his; he would see—oh, how could he endure it?—Lester Scott's handsome, arrogant countenance with an assurance written large upon it that no one (except himself and Rose) knew the dark secret; for while he might boast of a physical conquest he was not likely to incur the judgment of his young peers by admitting its tragic results. Rose was liked and respected too much for that; then in the last row, where there was more room for his long legs, would be Abe Williams himself. To these and to the class as a whole Gavin knew he must present his usual manner, earnest, penetrative, witty if there was occasion, and emotionally cogent as his subject matter demanded. With all his power he had tried to live up to his high ideals of teaching. The familiar warning, *publish or perish,* had not unduly influenced him, though he knew Devereux was working now on a book. The academic dictum he felt had more weight in universities and larger colleges. Although he realized that one day he might want to write, he felt his immediate business was to *teach,* and teach he did in a way that made students hasten to his class, even if it was the last one in the afternoon. The knowledge of this had borne him up during many stresses and strains, so now, *God help me to get through this day,* he thought.

As a matter of fact it proved to be easier than he had feared, for Lester Scott was absent as he frequently was. Rose, with a trifle more makeup than usual, looked beautifully normal, and Abe, slouching a bit in his chair, managed to be almost invisible behind those seated in the row ahead of him. The day passed, the last period was over and Gavin, after finishing some papers, went out to his car. He had told Bruce he was driving home, because his legs felt strangely unsteady under him and also because he didn't want to talk to the Judge just yet. When he reached the car he found Devereux waiting for him.

"How now, good sir?" the latter began in his blandest tone.

"Not so good," Gavin replied. "I'm still shook up. Heard anything more?"

"Not much, but I was talking to Bunny for a few minutes and she sort of sniffled around to the effect that she'd been to the Waring's for *tea* yesterday afternoon—God forbid that it might have been cocktails—and she said the President was unusually cheerful and she thought he just might have found a way out of the *ethical impasse*. Her words, not mine. Look, isn't that your pretty daughter over there?"

It was Rose, walking alone toward the campus entrance.

"Say," Devereux went on, somewhat

hesitantly, "wasn't she dating the Scott boy pretty heavily for a while?"

"Yes," Gavin's voice was casual. "But it broke up and I must say I was relieved."

"I'll bet you were. Well, in the classic phrase, I'll keep my nose to the ground. Bunny might really know something. I have an idea we'll be called in session again soon. Tomorrow maybe. Ah, in the immortal words: *Tomorrow and tomorrow and tomorrow . . .*"

"Get enough of them and you'll have a week," Gavin retorted with a grin, as he started the car.

He overtook Rose just beyond the entrance, walking slowly, apparently engaged in her own thoughts to the exclusion of everything else. "Could I give you a lift, Miss?" he asked politely as he slowed up. She raised her head and as she saw him her old smile flashed across her face. "*Could you?*" she said. "You're heaven sent. I looked for the car but I didn't see it. I thought you'd gone."

"Oh, somebody nabbed my usual parking spot. What kept you so late?"

"I finished up some lab work and then Miss Matthews cornered me to talk about the scenery for the play. I thought she'd *never* stop."

"How's the show going?"

"Well," Rose said consideringly, "better than I ever thought it would. It seemed to me the *dumbest* choice. I was all for Pinter's *Birthday Party* or something avant garde like that, if we could get the rights. Of course I realize the cast would have been too small, but the funny thing about *The Student Prince* is that it's so old it's new to everybody at college and it looks as though we're going to have a sell-out both nights, for I gather all the old folks in town are coming to renew their youth."

"How is Abe doing?"

"Oh, he's still stiff but better than he was at first, thank heaven. Of course his singing is . . ."

"Pretty good?"

"It's incredibly good, now that he's really loosened up and let his voice out. The thing that is worrying Miss Matthews and me, too, is that in front of an audience he may blow up in his big song. You know that one: 'Overhead the Moon Is Beaming.' "

"Oh, yes. Lovely thing."

"Well, you see, Abe's still nervous and as shy as a fawn even when we're rehearsing.

And if he would break on that song it would really ruin the play. It's a sort of high spot, you know."

"What he needs is confidence in himself," Gavin said, trying to keep his voice normal.

"Yes, of course. But you can't pour that into a person with a teaspoon."

"Rose," her father said steadily, "don't ask me how I know things. Any professor is at the end of a queer grapevine, but also I tried to help Abe a little once with his lines. The point is I have a strong suspicion that he would like to ask you for a date only he thinks you wouldn't go out with him."

"A *date*," Rose almost screamed. *"With me?* Well, he's quite right I wouldn't go out with him. That's the craziest thing I ever heard." She laughed, and it hurt Gavin's heart to hear her.

"I want to speak seriously of this possibility, my dear," he said, "so hear me through. I haven't talked with you about your problem since Friday night, but as you can imagine it is constantly in my mind and your mother's as we try to come to the best decision for your good. Now as to the play. It is vitally important under the circumstances that you present to the audience, which in a way means to the town, an image of beautiful, gifted, carefree girlhood taking your own lead with complete success. That success is absolutely dependent upon Abe's. If he 'blows up,' as you call it, it will practically ruin your whole role. We don't want that to happen. Nothing can give Abe confidence that a date with you can give. So I'm begging you, Rose, for your own sake, to go out with him if he invites you."

Rose made no answer. To Gavin's horror as he glanced at her he saw the tears running down her cheeks.

"Do you think he'll ask me?" she said chokingly at last.

"I don't know," Gavin said, "but I hope so."

There was silence between them then as they drew up to the house. Rose went upstairs at once, but came to dinner with fresh makeup and no sign of tears. Before the meal was ended the phone rang in the living room. Bruce answered while Gavin held his breath. He had the feeling that if Abe got his courage up to call at all it would be soon.

"For you, Rose," Bruce reported carelessly. "One of your swains but I didn't recognize his voice."

The family could not help overhearing Rose's conversation.

"Yes. Oh, yes? . . . I'm fine, thank you." Long pause, then, "Friday night? Why, I think I'm free then . . . I believe I would prefer the late movie . . . All right. Thank you. I'll be ready. Good-bye."

She returned to the table, her cheeks crimson. "Well, be it known to all and sundry that I am going to the movies Friday night with *Abe Williams.*" Her tone was pure scorn.

Bruce gave a yelp. "Yeah bo! That's a new one. But listen, gal. I'll tell you he's a good guy. Why are you going out with him, though, if you turn up your nose at him like that?"

"Oh, it's really on account of the show. We can talk over a few things. But I can't say I'm very thrilled at the prospect. He'll probably call for me in an ox-cart," and she excused herself and flounced out of the room.

Later when Bruce was alone with his father he spoke of Rose.

"She seems so edgy sometimes. Do you suppose she misses going out with Scott?"

"Could be," Gavin assented.

"He's got the fastest car in town and he's

a big spender. Of course all the girls flip over him, but when it comes to my sister, I'm just as glad he's not around any more.''

"You and I both."

Bruce looked right and left carefully. "Listen, Pop. You know one night at dinner Ian told about a girl fainting in his French class? Well, he was just telling me the latest dirt. It seems she's been hustled off to an aunt in California. You can imagine the talk among the kids. There's an awful lot of funny business going on, as of course you know. And it's not all amongst the young folks," he added seriously. "You've had John Partridge, haven't you?"

"I could hardly forget him. Every time he came in I wondered if we'd have room for the rest of the class."

"He's a big one all right, but Dad he's in trouble. He and I have been pretty good friends and I worry about him now. He's completely changed. I'm afraid he'll just plain freak out."

"What's wrong?"

"Well, you see everything in the family seemed O.K. until a couple of months ago, then they found out his father's been making it with some dame in the city and he wants a divorce. And this has just knocked John for a loop. He's reading Nietzsche and Sartre and all the *God-is-dead* stuff and he says he's a nihilist and he's going to quit college and he's going to try LSD and I don't know what all. I just wondered, Pop, if you could talk to him?''

"Why, my dear boy, what could I say? Or how could I make an occasion to say it if I did know what?''

"Well, I know it's awkward, but if I could get him to go in to see you someday after school he just might open up, and you do have a way with the fellahs. They know you're on the level with them and you know the score. If I can get him in, would you talk to him?''

"Of course, if he would want it. But I wouldn't like to make a bad matter worse by saying the wrong thing.''

"You wouldn't. You don't leave till around four-thirty, do you?''

"Not as a rule.''

"Let me see what I can do. He's up tight all right, I can tell you. He's always talked a lot about his father. Been proud of him and all that. Well, thanks, Pop, it's worth a try.''

Slightly against Devereux's prediction there was no faculty meeting called until Friday. Then Dr. Waring, wearing an expression of extreme benevolence, brought up a number of matters: one was the practically certain sell-out for the play, the proceeds of which were to go to the Library Fund. "Very gratifying," he kept repeating; another was the idea that the faculty reception given annually for the Seniors the first week of June might be changed to a combination with the alumni luncheon, becoming a reception and buffet for all, on Commencement Day. This produced animated discussion while Gavin squirmed in his chair. No conclusion was reached but a committee appointed; the name of the Commencement speaker, much touted by Dr. Waring and unknown to most of the faculty, was presented.

The subject of the music for the Senior Prom brought forth the liveliest controversy. Dr. Waring was strongly opposed to a whole evening of what he called "ear-destroying cacophony of sound." Some sort of curb should be put on this for the sake of the dignity of Marsden. Gavin finally raised his voice.

"I have a suggestion," he said. "The Seniors are young people removed by much *more* than a generation from us and our tastes. I think their committee should select the band, orchestra or whatever they want and that they should have rock and roll or Tijuana Brass or any earsplitting stuff they all *like*. It's their Prom. But I would make one stipulation: that during the evening there must be played two beautiful waltzes. This would be good for them without spoiling their fun. Have one for the closing number. 'Till we meet again,' for instance. They all know that. Well that would be my strong recommendation.

To his surprise and pleasure, the whole faculty agreed with him. Dr. Waring, knowing when he was beaten, fell into line, dwelling heavily upon the waltzes, suggesting "The Blue Danube," for the first one.

At last he folded his little paper list and in what seemed almost an offhand manner said, "Oh, I wish to inform you that at a meeting of the trustees on Wednesday night I brought before them the problem that several of our Seniors, *several,*" he repeated distinctly, "will for one reason or another not be able to complete their year's work by Commencement Day. After a thorough and I might add a very intelligent discussion it was unanimously agreed that these young people should receive their diplomas along with the others. However, they will be told privately and it will also be announced in Chapel that their diplomas are to be returned to the office and held there until the work is made up, at which time the proper signatures will be placed on them and they will be given to their owners. There was particular pleasure on the part of the trustees over this plan since as you know the long illness of Sarah Means, a local girl, has driven her now to work harder than she is able. John Daley's accident also has held him back. So, the trustees are entirely satisfied over the proposed arrangement and I hope you as the faculty will be also. Any questions?" A very slight pause, and then, "We will now adjourn to work over other details of Commencement at a later date."

There was general quiet as the meeting broke up. Devereux managed to walk with Gavin until they reached their cars.

"And what say you to that, Sir Galahad?" he inquired.

"Relief, that's what I say."

"But the neatness of it! I swear if Waring had pulled a white rabbit from his coat pocket it couldn't have been a better piece of magic. Look at it! Old Scott himself completely content. Son receiving diploma among all the others. That's all he wants.

116

What the hell! Who needs a diploma afterward anyway? College reputation unstained, student body satisfied that all is above board. No selling out for money. I tell you, Gavin, the thing's perfect. But it's too smart by a long shot for Waring to dream up. Do you know what I think? I believe Bunny on her virtuous spinster couch one night thought this whole thing out. She didn't like to sell her soul any more than we did. But she's smart. Got her Doctorate when she was thirty, I've heard. You know I told you she sounded the other day as if she knew something. Well, I'd say she did."

"That just could be," Gavin assented. "As to the Means girl and John Daley, they were heading toward a passing mark anyway."

Devereux was still engrossed with his theme. "Yes, but they'll be glad of a little respite and they were absolutely necessary to this scheme. Oh, good old Bunny! She saved us all from the mouth of the lion. And you know, Gavin, she's not so old at that. Maybe fortyish. The trouble with her is that she's never had what the song calls 'One Night of Love.' "

"How do *you* know?"

"Ha! You ask a Frenchman that? It's

117

written all over her. She deserves a recompense for what she's done."

"For what you *think* she's done."

"She done it all right. What we have to do for her, Gavin, in return, is to get her a *lover*. It will make her over, stop her nose twitching even. She'd blossom like the autumn rose. What do you say?"

"I'd say you're indecent. I respect Bunny."

"Well, so do I. And I wasn't intimating that either you or I were to have an *affair* with her. We're good family men, but there ought to be somebody . . . by God, what about Schneider? He stuck his neck out with you on this thing and next to you he'll be the most relieved. And he's a bachelor! Now if we can only start a little something . . ."

"Count me out on this," Gavin said, turning to his car. He couldn't say that he was already so deeply engaged in a romantic intrigue that his heart was all but torn out by the roots because of it. "I think you're crazy and you'd better be careful you don't burn your fingers. Or anyone else's," he added.

"I won't," Devereux said airily. "I'm a historian, or supposed to be, and it's made me extremely sensitive to the unusual manifestations of sex within the framework of propinquity. Now, I intend to do a little finagling, and you, my sainted friend, might remember the project in your orisons. That won't in any way besmirch your character."

"I wish," Gavin retorted irritably, "that you wouldn't treat me as a cross between a sissy and an angel. I'm human enough."

"Now don't get huffy. I think you're a completely honest man, and they don't grow so thick on the bushes. So long now. I'm suddenly in love with my own idea!"

Gavin started his car, as usual half angry, half amused at Devereux. But the latter signed to him to wait.

"Look," he said, lowering his voice, "it mightn't do any harm to throw a sop to Cerberus now and then. Just a thought."

"Waring?"

"Who else? He was certainly in an unctuous mood today; but he never forgets anything and you *were,* shall we say, rather outspoken last week."

Gavin stared at him. "You know you're a good friend, Devereux, and I appreciate it. However, I'm not so good at *sops* and besides I don't think Waring could hold last week against me since all is so beautifully fixed up now. He must know himself that I only spoke the truth then."

"That's the trouble. As Shakespeare puts it:

A slander we can bravely bear;
It is the truth that hurts.

"Well, skip the gutter," he called cheerfully as he moved away.

Gavin's relief over the outcome of the problem of Lester Scott's graduation was so great that his mind passed completely over Devereux's last warning. The important fact to him was that he was free now to concentrate upon Rose. And Abe. This was the night of the date, and what would come of it he was afraid to contemplate. When he got home he managed a few minutes alone in the kitchen with Cecily. While the college problem had been dwarfed by their personal one, it had still loomed as a dark backdrop to their thinking. So, he was glad to have one bit of good news to tell.

"Oh, Gavin, I'm so relieved for you!" she cried. "By the way, Bob called to say he'd stop in tonight, if we weren't busy."

"Fine! I'll call him at once. I wanted an excuse for being up when Rose gets home and this will give us a good one. She's never inhibited in front of him, so we'll get the news just as if we were alone.''

Dinner was normal enough, though Rose was silent. The boys both wanted the car but Bruce relinquished it after some discussion in which Ian pointed out that Bruce didn't have to impress his girl but he did. "And I shined her up top to bottom," he said. "I mean the car." And Rose joined in the ever-ready laughter.

Bob St. Clair arrived before Rose left. He was a handsome man, tall, slender and muscular, with dark hair and eyes. He came of old Marsden stock, his father and grandfather both having been judges. So Gavin twitted him on his breeding as being out of Blackstone by Corpus Juris. He had both suavity and wit as well as brains and had risen so rapidly in his profession that it was a foregone conclusion by most that he would reach a judgeship himself eventually. But while on the social side he was accounted the town's most eligible bachelor and duly squired all the older and younger debutantes both in Marsden and in the city, he seemed impervious to serious romance. He and Gavin had taken to each other from their first meeting and the friendship had deepened with the years. He was "Uncle Bob" to the children and the lively

McAllister home, in which he was a frequent and casual guest, seemed to fill a lonely void in his heart which his own well-run and elegant menage could not do. He sat down with satisfaction now in a big chair and complained that his own were not so comfortable and he couldn't see why.

"Oh, I can tell you," Cecily said quickly. "When two big boys keep dropping their considerable weight constantly into a chair, the cushion is bound to get softer and the springs more—shall I say—resilient. If they hold up at all. Your chairs are not used enough. That's the reason."

"Maybe. That's a pretty dress, Cecily. A new one? It brings out all the dimples."

It was a robin's egg blue and the strain upon Cecily's heart manifested itself by heightened color. Her eyes were very bright and she felt she must marshal all her self-control or they might overflow.

"Mercy no. You must have seen it before. But Bob, please don't give me compliments. This is not one of my *dimply* days. I'm likely to burst into a flood of tears at any moment. Everything went wrong. I broke my favorite vase this morning when I was arranging the flowers. I fell down the back steps. Oh, nothing's hurt but my pride. Then I baked a cake and *it* fell. And when I stopped at school for Cissie her teacher tells me she's loafing again after a phenomenal A or two. She just sits blissfully 'enjoying the atmosphere,' as Miss Jackson says, but with no intention of working if she can avoid it. She's going to pass with a squeeze. It's silly to worry at her age but it does bother me a bit."

"And besides?" Bob said quizzically.

"Oh, you know too much about women! Why should you think there is a *besides* today?" She felt like an actress playing a role.

"Come on. Out with it."

"Well, if you must know, I felt a little hurt that Gavin and I didn't get an invitation for the Carter cocktail party next week." *As though it mattered,* she thought.

"If it's any comfort to you, neither did I."

"You don't mean it!"

"Yep. Lots of people got left out, I hear. And what I thought is this. Liz Carter is such a nit-wit that she probably mailed half the cards and forgot the rest. It was supposed to be a big wing-ding and she's always so vague she'd be sure to get mixed up somehow. By the way, where's the old man?"

"Oh, he's out at the car. Ian is taking it

tonight and Gavin doesn't think he's too expert a driver yet so he always double checks things . . . oh, here he is now.''

Gavin came in, slapped Bob on the shoulder and sank down on the sofa.

"Gosh, it's good to see you under more pleasant circumstances than the last time. Have you seen Billy since? I must run in soon.''

"Yes, I stopped by yesterday. He looks pretty seedy but he was full of talk. The great trouble is he doesn't eat enough. Just drinks. He gets his check the first of the month, you know, from the New York bank, and I think we'll have to try to snare enough from it to lay in some food for him. Maybe you could manage that better than I could.''

"I'll try. We'll have to see to it, for he's not getting any younger. Well, what's the state of the law?''

"About the same as education, I imagine,'' Bob grinned. "Could be im- proved.''

There were steps on the porch and the doorbell rang.

"Young Scott, I suppose?'' Bob inquired.

"No,'' Cecily said quietly as Gavin went to the door. "That's broken up.''

When Abe entered the room his embarrassment was acute. He was properly dressed, however, in jacket and slacks, and Gavin had seen not an ox-cart but a very decent-looking car in front of the house.

"I don't think you've met my wife," he was saying cordially to the boy. "Cecily, this is Abe Williams, one of my students, and this is Mr. St. Clair, one of our good friends."

Cecily shook hands warmly, as did Bob, while Abe managed a few stammering words in reply to their greetings.

"Sit down, Abe," Gavin said, "and I'll call Rose. Girls always make a point of being late, it seems. Eh, Bob?"

"Oh," Cecily put in with her quick smile, "it's really become a sort of status symbol. The lateness, I mean. One of Rose's friends says she never starts to dress until she hears her date come in. But Rose isn't quite as bad as that. And when it's the movies she really like to be there when the picture starts, as I'm sure you do, Abe."

"Yes, I do. I mean no . . . I mean it really doesn't make any difference." Abe's face was flushed and the color mounted as Rose ran down the stairs and into the room.

"Oh, hello, Uncle Bob," she said, kissing St. Clair lightly. "It's good to see you.

Hello, Abe. I suppose we'd better start, hadn't we?"

Abe had risen when he saw St. Clair do so and now with a general good-bye added to that of Rose, they went out.

When the footsteps were heard on the walk, Bob looked curiously at Cecily.

"What's the pitch here?" he asked. "That boy doesn't seem to be Rose's style. Certainly not after Lester Scott. You know I had rather pictured a wedding after Commencement and Rose the mistress of the Scott mansion. And how she would grace it!" he added.

Gavin with a glance at Cecily, spoke quickly. "Oh, Rose is mad at Lester, and I'm sure the bust-up is permanent. He's an arrogant young pup and I imagine he throws his weight around a little too much. As to this boy, he and Rose have the leading roles in the Senior play, so they've been sort of thrown together. He's a nice chap and a very bright one, but as you could see, terribly shy."

"Yes," Bob agreed. "I thought for a while he was going to put his hands in his shoes. He's got a good face, though. As to Lester," he went on, "as I say I was watching developments with interest for they would certainly have made the world's most handsome couple. He's a reckless young Jehu, though. He's all but lost his license more than once. Loren always gets round the Judge, somehow. I think the boy's a little on the wild side, but I always thought a good wife would tame him down. Well, Rose need never lack for suitors, that's sure. Oh, talk to me about anything, you two. I've had the devil of a hard week and I'm sick of courts and cases. What's that you're making, Cecily?''

His dark eyes rested upon her intently as she sat with the light shining down on her hair while her hands were busy with some yarns.

"It's needlepoint for a dining room chair seat. The first of six and I'm a very slow worker. You might call this the triumph of hope over experience," she added lightly.

If, she was thinking, they could only tell Bob the whole terrible problem and have the benefit of his shrewd wisdom and knowledge of the world! She looked across at Gavin with the question upon her face. He shook his head and then said quickly, "I told her she was foolish to attempt this, but after all who can stop the creative urge?"

There was easy laughter and talk which

wandered into various fields until the clock had struck eleven and Bob rose at last to go.

"Oh, stick around a little longer," Gavin said. "We want to be up when Rose gets back to see how she made out with Abe, and you'll give us a good excuse."

Bob relaxed in his chair. "As you well know I never need to be coaxed to stay . . . Isn't that a car stopping now?"

It was. They could hear a door slam and footsteps on the walk and the porch, but no voices. Rose burst into the room.

"Give me a book to lend Abe, Daddy. *Anything!*" she whispered half hysterically.

Gavin reached to the shelf behind him, and drew out a volume at random. He glanced at it as he handed it to her. "Omar. That ought to hold him for a while."

They could hear a muffled "Good-night and I enjoyed the picture," then retreating steps as Rose re-entered the room and flung herself down on a chair.

"The most *awful* thing happened! The most *ghastly* thing! We went to the Odeon, for our crowd hardly ever goes there and I thought nobody would see us. On the way out in the lobby we heard Kat Hastings. You can always hear her a mile away. And she said, 'Would you look at Rose McAllister with *Honest Abe!* She must be hard up for a date.' I didn't know what I was doing, but I was so mad I had to say something, so I just said good and loud, 'Remind me to lend you that book, Abe, when we get home.' "

"Good for you," Gavin said. "That was an unspeakably rude thing for the Hastings girl to do, but I think you handled it well."

"What did you say to Abe when you got in the car?" Cecily asked breathlessly.

"We didn't say anything for a while and then I told him I didn't think anyone should be ashamed to have the same nickname as Lincoln. And he thanked me and said I was pretty quick to think of the book business."

"You were," Gavin said. "I'm proud of you."

"But you haven't heard the *worst of it!*" Rose exclaimed. All at once her eyes overflowed. "Before we got to the house he asked me for another date next week! And what could I *do?* What could I *say* after what happened, I felt so sorry for him. But here I'll be stuck with him again. Oh, it's too much! Daddy, you never should have gotten me into this. I'm just sick over the whole thing. You've no idea what he's like, Uncle Bob. He's clear out of it. He simply doesn't *know anything!*"

"Well," St. Clair said calmly, "he may be better, at that, than a boy who knows too much."

At the words Rose looked at him, startled, and drew a quick breath while her face slowly flamed scarlet. Without another word she left the room and they could hear her running up the stairs and closing the door.

Nobody spoke as Bob slowly put out his cigarette.

"You are my closest friends," he said, "and I love your children almost as though they were my own. If I can ever be of service to you or any of them . . ."

He broke off as he rose. "Heavens! I didn't mean to stay so long, but I've enjoyed it. Don't wear yourself out with that chair-seat business, Cecily. And Gavin, will you take a look at Billy one of these days? You're his idol. He merely tolerates me, as his lawyer," he laughed.

There were normal good-nights at the door, then Gavin came back and slumped down where he had been sitting. The bright yarn had dropped from Cecily's fingers.

"If anything could have made me more utterly miserable," he said, "than I was already it was Rose's account of the evening. I was somehow counting . . ." Then suddenly he sat up straight. "But listen! There's something we're forgetting. That boy had the *guts* to ask her for another date even after what he heard. Why, that shows *character!*"

Cecily did not respond at once. She was looking behind him. "Gavin, I think Bob put two and two together tonight. I believe, especially from what he said at the last, that he suspects something."

They sat in silence until Gavin said very low, "How long do we have before we must act?"

"I think about six weeks."

"Oh, darling," he burst out, "are you *sure* about it all? Could there possibly be a mistake?"

She raised a white face. "I'm afraid there's been no mistake," she said.

Four

THE INVITATION TO dinner at the Devereuxs' came as a distinct surprise. Marie was French, charming and witty with the faintest air of condescension toward the other faculty wives. She made no bones of the fact that she considered her husband's talents wasted in Marsden, but unfortunately his nature was inimical to change so he was content to remain where he was, teaching, reading and writing his book on the life and times of Charlemagne on the side.

"Now what do you suppose this means?" Cecily asked as she showed Gavin the elegantly monogrammed card. " 'Just a little dinner for a few of our faculty friends.' The last time I tried that Marie seemed bored to death. We've always gotten on well and I like her, but I do think she's *devious*. There's something behind this."

"Now, now," Gavin retorted, "don't look

a gift invitation in the mouth. It will do us good to go and forget our troubles a little. I must say when we finally got to the Carters' party I almost forgot we had a problem. How does Rose seem to you now?"

"Oh, she's working feverishly both for her exams and for the play. I hear her vocalizing in season and out, and it does seem as though her voice is growing stronger. Of course its quality is always lovely. But Gavin dear . . ."

"Yes, darling."

"What if at the end she absolutely refuses to agree to our plan? What could we *do?*"

Gavin's lips set in a firm line. "I don't think the poor child will have much choice," he said, and the words were more tender than stern.

When the night for Abe's second date came around, he entered the living room much less frightened and more relaxed than the first time, and when Rose appeared in the doorway he was on his feet at once.

That boy learns fast, Gavin thought as he watched them leave. He and Cecily had not meant to be waiting when they returned but Gavin had put in a full evening's work in the study and come down to the kitchen where

Cecily was making coffee. When the young people got back Rose came straight to the kitchen and Abe followed.

"Well, how was the show?" Gavin asked.

"Pretty good," Rose answered.

"I thought so, too," Abe echoed, smiling.

"We were just about to have a little snack. Will you join us?"

"Not me," Rose said. "We stopped at The Pantry after the movie and I couldn't eat another thing."

"Coffee, Abe?"

"No, thanks. I've got to get going."

They heard thanks and good-nights at the door, then Rose came back and sank down on a kitchen stool.

"How did it go this time, dear?" Cecily asked eagerly.

"Oh, better in a way. There weren't any *audible* remarks. Just raised eyebrows. I was determined to brazen the thing out, so I suggested we go into The Pantry for a pizza afterwards. I hope I didn't break the poor guy up. We ran into some other kids there who are in the play so we had plenty to talk about. There's no problem about the boys. Abe gets along well with them."

"I think you've done a very fine thing, Rose," her father said. "You can see the change in Abe already. I'm sure you needn't worry now about his cracking up in his role."

"Well," Rose said tonelessly, as she got up, "don't ever say I didn't do my part for good old Marsden."

The letter from Aunt Het came the very morning of the Devereuxs' dinner. And while, as Gavin pointed out, it was only another step along the strange road they were preparing for Rose to travel, yet it represented concrete encouragement, a necessary and firm foothold, as it were, without which the way would be impossible. So, cheered by this, even as they realized the limitations of their own judgment and the lack of conformity to it which they might soon encounter, they still had enough warmth from the letter to make their social smiles as they entered the Devereux home not all counterfeit.

For Aunt Het had written as eagerly as her Scottish restraint would permit. She had never gotten over the loss of Gavin himself and to have his daughter and her husband there and maybe a *bairn* later on as he had suggested would be nigh heaven to her for she would admit she got lonely betimes and liked a bit stir in the house. As Gavin would remember there were just the two rooms and scullery downstairs and the two up. Lately she'd been using the one downstairs for her own bedroom but the kitchen was big and cozy. The long horsehair sofa still stood behind the table and there were plenty rockers. She always shined up the stove with a bit of velvet so it looked nice and the brass rail would be just the thing to dry hippens on later. She still did all the rough work in the scullery. The big miss to the young folks would be a bathroom but there was a nice wash-bowl set upstairs and the lavat'ry was under cover behind the kitchen. All she could say was that if they would come she'd do her best to make them comfortable, and if they would let her know about the time she'd give the house the turn-out of its life to freshen things up for them. She sent love to all.

So Gavin and Cecily entered the Devereux home with a small relief in their hearts. The house itself had a charming and unusual decor, the walls being stone white with green draperies and great jars of forsythia on either side of the fireplace. There were other yellow accents too, including Marie's dress which somehow made her dark hair and eyes seem brighter. There were only six guests: the Copleys, Lee and Sarah, he of the modern languages department, were there already and in a moment in came *Schneider and Bunny.* Marie greeted them almost effusively.

"Oh, Dr. Schneider, how very kind of you to pick up Dr. Foster. It might have been a little out of the way for any of the others. Do go on up to my room, Hilda, and make yourself comfortable. One nice thing about a faculty party," she went on ushering Schneider into the living room where Devereux welcomed him, "is that there are no introductions necessary. It's all *en famille,* as it were."

Schneider, who Gavin knew was not often invited out, acknowledged the greeting with evident pleasure as a large, friendly St. Bernard might have received a pat on the head. He was still standing when Bunny, without her hat and coat, appeared in the doorway, and his eyes behind their thick lenses stared at her unbelievingly. There was no gasp of astonishment of course from so sophisticated a group, but all looked toward her, even as Schneider, with a startled pleasure. For Bunny was transformed. And yet the changes were so subtle that it was hard to see how they had effected a sort of transmutation. Ever since she had been at

Marsden she had worn her hair, the ash blond which longest defies the gray, in a bun at the back of her neck. So she still did. But now, pinned across it was a blue velvet bow the color of her dress. She was wearing lipstick which she did not usually do, and where her skirts as a rule were nearer her ankles than her knees, the one she was wearing had been shortened to a decently modern length. And because of this her feet in high-heeled pumps were distinctly visible as being small and pretty. That was all. And yet it was enough to change Dr. Foster, head of the Latin and Greek department, into a woman.

It was a very clever hand back of this, Gavin was thinking as he helped himself to a cocktail from the tray Devereux was passing. *I would guess a French hand which knew just where to stop with Bunny.*

He glanced at his hostess as her bright eyes swept the room, missing nothing. Without ever overstepping the bounds of decorum she had a certain beguiling grace which made every man to whom she spoke feel flattered and in a sense much more brilliant than the facts would warrant.

Dinner, as always there, was delicious and Marie managed with Gallic vivacity to keep the conversation lively. Had they ever read of the famous Howling Monkeys? She had always supposed they were called that because they howled all the time. But no, it was only when another monkey was threatening to invade their territory. She had just come across this book. This led to a lengthy discussion of the territorial imperative, wandering off into primates in general until Schneider brought laughter and comment from the women when he averred that a gorilla was the only creature who could actually be stared out of countenance!

"Even if I tried it I'd still prefer to have a few bars between us," he added.

The Copleys had seen a really good Western movie. A regular rip-snorter, but fascinating. However, the question was whether Europeans and even some English might feel this was actually a portrayal of a section of present day American life. Conversation waxed entertainingly hot over this until at last it settled down into local gossip, omitting reference to the Carters' cocktail party at which neither Bunny nor Schneider had been present and skirting carefully unsavory episodes of the town about which everyone had heard.

"I met your protégé, Billy King, on the

street yesterday, Gavin,'' Devereux said. ''He wasn't walking too straight but he was sober enough to stop me and inquire into the history of my name. It seems as though anything French is the password to his soul. When he got onto Paris I thought I was never going to get away. Did he ever really do any painting?''

''He did, indeed. If he had been willing to discipline himself and stick to it I think he might have been a real artist. He has one picture on his wall that I admire greatly. He's rather evasive about it but I'm sure it's his own work.''

''It is always unfortunate,'' Marie said sweetly as she gave the signal to rise, ''when a man lacks ambition, n'est-ce pas?''

There's one for her husband, Gavin thought with inner amusement as they all returned to the drawing room for coffee and liqueurs. And it was here that Devereux himself, quietly and firmly, set the pace for the conversation that was to follow.

''Now here we are,'' he began, ''a group of presumably intelligent people, a little above average shall we say without vanity, so we should be interested in discussing just what part increased intelligence is going to play in the future of mankind. To put it bluntly, are we going to outsmart ourselves right out of existence? Or can the activity of the brain somehow be curbed—sort of a thus-far-canst-thou-go-and-no-further kind of thing—to save us from our own self-destruction?"

"Never," said Schneider at once in his deep voice. "We must have freedom of intelligence and accept the consequences. Freedom in any area carries a risk and we have to take it."

"But Dr. Schneider," Cecily put in eagerly, "if we knew right now that future discoveries here and possibly on other planets would end in our little earth's being burned to a crisp, would you say going ahead with them was *right?*"

Schneider considered and then said slowly. "I would not say *right* was the word, but inevitable. You see we are dealing with a force here, greater than the atom bomb. And it can't be controlled and shouldn't be even if it were possible. It's man's brain that is involved. It's . . ."

"Man's unconquerable mind," Gavin quoted.

"That's it exactly. Just what I was trying to get at, only I don't know the poets. Well, I've talked a good deal for me. I'd

141

better keep quiet."

"Not for too long," said Devereux, "we may need you again. As Dr. Waring always says, 'We wish for a concerted opinion.' " He laughed and the others joined.

"Here's mine, for what it's worth," Gavin began. "I've always wondered in a blundering sort of way if the discovery of the atom bomb—and I suppose that's what we're all thinking about—could not be countered with another kind of discovery which would, in a sense, contain it or nullify its danger."

"There are all the beneficent uses of atomic power. Don't forget them," Copley said. "Or is that what you're thinking of?"

"No," said Gavin, "they aren't enough to remove danger. What I meant was an equal and contrary reaction by the intelligence. An opposing *force* of a saving nature, if such a thing could be."

"But there *is*, Mr. McAllister." Everyone turned in surprise toward Bunny, for it was she who was speaking. Her face, all earnestness, was becomingly flushed, and free from any twitchings. "There is such a force if we could only educate people to it." They were all watching her intently as she leaned forward and went on speaking, not hesitantly as usual but with the words tumbling over each other. "I know it may sound foolish to you at first, but do hear me through and think about it. Now love as a concrete emotion is necessary for the continuance of the species, you'd all agree. Therefore we could say it is essential to the survival of mankind. Its wider application, of course, is kindness and understanding of others, *empathy,* if you wish. If an atom bomb is ever dropped again it will be because of enmity between peoples. But suppose instead there was a powerful development of what we might call a *social morality* which would include all these positive feelings; there would never be an atomic war. Well," she ended, now rather embarrassed, "that's the way it seems to me. And *there's* your counteracting force, Mr. McAllister."

Devereux had been slouching in his chair, his eyelids half closed but his expression intent. He spoke first now. "I think Bu—, Dr. Foster, you are entirely right from the first to last. The only question I would raise is how we are going to achieve this *social morality,* as you term it. The idea of loving our neighbor is not exactly a new concept, and we haven't gotten very far with it."

"I know," Bunny agreed. "It's so old we

pay no attention to it. But it's never been so desperately necessary as it is today. And I think the only way it could be done is through education. And that's where we all come in."

Marie laughed. "My dear Hilda, you can't *teach* love."

All at once the room blazed into heated discussion. The only problem was for each to be heard.

"A beautiful idea, but completely impractical."

"Now wait a minute. Suppose you started in the lower grades teaching children to be kind and understanding and all that, the way you teach them reading and writing . . ."

"And kept on up to college level? What would you call it then? Course in *empathy?* Wouldn't work."

"But I tell you there's something in this . . ."

So it went, back and forth, pro and con, as the hours grew later and then earlier, when a new seriousness settled upon the group.

"There is this," Copley said slowly. He was a youngish man with thick blond hair and gray eyes that looked levelly at you. "The universities and colleges have always made a point of staying clear of anything like a moral issue. But why should they? They are the intellectual leaders. Theoretically they ought to be molding the youth. Now I'd be willing to bet that if they all began to concern themselves with this matter of *empathy* or social morality or whatever you want to call it, the campus riotings and all the student uprisings would stop. This is what the kids want. This is what they're blundering after. Of course we don't have that kind of trouble here, but there's plenty of it across the country, God knows. And I think it's dangerous."

At the end it was Schneider who looked solemnly through his thick glasses.

"But suppose we were all agreed to try something like this here in Marsden next fall. It's a little late to start now. What could we do? How would we go about it? And would there be a chance of the idea spreading if we did? We're a pretty small institution relatively."

"I think it *would* spread," Copley said. "If we were all earnest enough. Take the matter of a joke. Someone tells it to us here today and by next week it's all over California. That's not a parallel case I admit, but it illustrates our present incredible communication. There are all sorts of ways this idea could be made to spread to larger colleges and universities, but my first question is like Dr. Schneider's, how could we go about the thing ourselves in the first place?"

Devereux's face had a quizzical expression. "I'm just wondering," he said, "if perhaps any of us has been practicing this without knowing it. I would wager that McAllister here has been dropping a moral now and then along with his English. How about it, Gavin?"

Gavin flushed to the roots of his hair. "Oh, now, why pick on me? We probably all try to point up a truth when we see it."

"But give us an example," Schneider said earnestly. "Something concrete. I'm in the worst place of any of you if we should as a faculty try to do something about this. How can I teach love and understanding starting in a laboratory?"

"They can be taught anywhere," Bunny put in gently.

"Come, Gavin," Devereux went on. "Give us a sample of the way you go about this. Don't be bashful."

"But I am," Gavin declared. "In the first place I can't just pull a bit of conversation, maybe two or three weeks old, out of my hat, as it were. And the only thing I could cite to you is not exactly apropos to what we've been talking about, I'm afraid. It just deals with the relations between two individuals."

"That's good enough," said Devereux. "As I understand this business that's where it all has to begin. Go ahead, Gavin. *Give with it!*"

Gavin was plainly embarrassed. "I couldn't quote this in every group but those of us here who are married are pretty solidly married. However, we all know the divorce statistics. What disturbs me is the number of young or young middle-aged couples who break up. So, in the remote hope that it may someday be of use to them I make every student who goes through my classes commit to memory, among other things, two verses from one of Tennyson's songs."

After a reluctant pause in which the room was quiet, he spoke slowly and with feeling.

As thro' the land at eve we went,
And pluck'd the ripen'd ears,
We fell out, my wife and I,
O, we fell out, I know not why,
And kiss'd again with tears.

*And blessings on the falling out
That all the more endears,
When we fall out with those we love,
And kiss again with tears!* . . .

There were a few seconds of silence. Marie was the one who broke it. "Thank you, Mr. McAllister. That, I'm ashamed to say, is new to me and I think beautiful. It may help more young people than you dream and may not do any of us old marrieds any harm either."

"And as to us," Cecily said rising, "I think it's time we left. We've paid you the highest compliment a hostess can have, Marie, in staying on till this hour. It's been the most interesting evening I've had in years."

There was the usual pleasant flurry of thanks and good-byes with here and there a deeper note creeping in about the evening's conversation. They all saw Schneider help Bunny down the steps with extreme care. When they were back in their own car Cecily spoke eagerly.

"Gavin, do you think there is really any chance of Bunny's idea being put into practice? Educationally, I mean."

"I don't know. Of course we were all a bit

carried away by our own eloquence tonight but the fact is that she made out a good case. To love our neighbors would really save the world. And I agree with her that education is the only way it can ever be achieved. But it's a big job to tackle, and while we were practicing a cult of love, a less civilized nation might gobble us up. We'd have to take that chance."

"I'd be ashamed to confess this to anybody but you, but I don't really know the difference between *sympathy* and *empathy.*"

"Oh, they are really a good deal alike. I would say sympathy has more of pity in it, and empathy really means putting yourself in the other fellow's place. Understanding him, you know. If love were ever to save the world I should think empathy would be the most important."

"Thanks," Cecily said, and then as though putting semantics aside, she gave a small laugh. "I was right about Marie. I knew there was something behind this party. Maybe you didn't notice, but she's actually trying to bring Bunny and Schneider together."

"I'm not entirely blind."

"So you thought of it too? And *did* you see the bow on Bunny's hair and what it did

149

to her? It took off ten years at least. But who but Marie would have thought of it? I think it's called a Dior bow, but certainly not prevalent here. Wouldn't it be exciting if something really came of this? Oh, matchmaking is such . . . ." Then all at once she crumpled down in the seat and great breaths shook her.

"Don't, Cecily," Gavin said. "We've had a rest tonight from our problem and it's been good for us. Oh, don't cry, my darling. *There's always a way.*"

At four-thirty the next day, as Gavin was putting papers into his briefcase, the door of the classroom opened and John Partridge entered. He was a handsome boy—all six feet four, two hundred pounds of him—and the football hero of the college. He came slowly toward the desk as Gavin went cordially to meet him.

"Come in, John. I'm glad to see you."

"I suppose you know," the boy said hesitantly, his face set, "that Bruce is responsible for my coming in. I don't think I ought to, actually, for the thing on my mind isn't very nice to say to you."

"You can say anything to me you like, John," Gavin replied. "Will you sit down?"

"No, thanks. Bruce said he told you what

has happened to me . . . to us. After the first awful shock about my . . . father, it just suddenly hit me that maybe that's the way it is. Nobody looking at *our* family would ever have dreamed there was anything wrong. So maybe all men my father's age either do what he's done—and of course a lot of them do—or *want* to even if they stick. It's just knocked the whole bottom out of marriage for me. I know I oughtn't to say this but I felt I had to find out the truth if I could, whatever it was."

Gavin stood quiet for a moment, while the boy watched him, then very slowly he said, "I can only speak for myself of course but I'm quite sure I'm not unique. I'll tell you, man to man, how it is with me. From the first time I met my wife, I've never *wanted* another woman."

John looked at him steadily, then said, "Thanks, Professor," and started toward the door.

Gavin called after him. "I'm so terribly sorry for your unhappiness. If you wish I'll be glad to talk with you. I'd like to help you."

The boy turned with a half-smile. "You have," he said. And went out.

Well, Gavin thought as he picked up his

briefcase, that's about the shortest interview I ever had. He had told Bruce that he and Rose could drive home as he himself wanted to walk. He felt like the exercise today and also he wanted to stop to see the Judge and tell him the latest developments, such as they were. He had already reported his first conversation with Abe.

"Well," the old man began as Gavin reached the small porch where the Judge was sitting, "I'd just decided if you didn't stop in again today I'd have to use the telephone, a device of the devil, if ever there was one. Let's go into the library an' set. You're lookin' better, that's a help."

But *he* isn't, Gavin thought. The Judge looked white and old and seemed to make more of a business even of sitting down, once they reached the library, than he usually did.

"Now," he said, "what's been goin' on? Does Rosie know yet about the plan?"

"Good heavens, no! We have to move slowly with this if we move at all. She still doesn't think much of Abe but she has had two dates with him."

He told the Judge in detail about these and then drew a paper from his pocket. "This came yesterday from the aunt I told you about. I'd better read it to you for the writing is pretty old-fashioned.''

As he read he could see the Judge's face relax, and at the end he chuckled.

''I like that. Nothin' fancy about her, but good common sense. Rosie'll be safe with her if we just get her there. An' that word *hippens!*'' He laughed and Gavin was glad to hear the sound. ''I haven't come across that one since I was a boy. An old Scotch woman lived near us an' if she thought I was gettin' too big feelin' she'd say, 'Now, now, mind the bushes ain't dry yet your *hippens* hung on!' Well, what do you do next? Seems to me you've come quite a ways already.''

''I feel that too. So much so that I'm half scared. Things almost too coincidental. The biggest hurdle is yet to come. That is Rose's own feelings. I'll use all my persuasion and what authority I have, but, Judge, if she absolutely refuses to marry Abe, what can we do? We can't in the old sense 'sell her down the river.' We'll have to use the other expedient.''

''Stop!'' the old man said. ''Don't consider anything else now but the present plan. I've had a long life to learn to smell things out ahead of time. I used to do it on the bench. I tell you now, this is going to work. So, just keep your tail up and go ahead. Is she having any more dates with the boy?"

"I don't know. Of course they'll be seeing each other at rehearsals. The play is two weeks from Friday. Why don't you come with us? I got extra tickets before the sell-out. Everyone who has seen or heard any of it thinks it's going to be quite a hit."

"Thanks. I'll wait and see how my joints are behaving. I'd like to see little Rosie . . ."

Gavin got up quickly. "Look," he said, "I've got to leave right away, for I want to run in to see how Billy King is getting along. I've been neglecting him lately, I'm afraid."

"Another *duty call,* eh?"

Gavin turned sharply and his face was stern.

"Don't ever again call my visits to you *duty calls,* Judge," he said, "or they'll stop."

To his surprise the old man's face crinkled up with pleasure. "Ha! Got your dander up, eh? Well, it sounded good to me and you needn't stop the visits. Just make another soon."

Gavin relaxed and smiled as he went off, remembering how once again the Judge had, in his earnestness, for the most part forgotten his grammar revolt.

When he got to Billy's door he heard the rise and fall of a voice inside—not a good sign. But when Billy ushered him in he found his friend practically sober.

"I've just been reciting some poetry," Billy explained. "You know once in a while it's as exhilarating as a shot of whiskey. But you wouldn't know anything about the whiskey, Mac, would you?"

"Oh, I guess maybe I could recognize the taste," Gavin grinned, "but what poem were you saying?"

" 'Dover Beach.' One of my favorites. I'll bet your students never heard of Matthew Arnold. He's gone out of style."

"What do you mean never heard of him? What kind of a college professor do you think I am? When we read 'Dover Beach,' though, I always have to explain the word *shingles*. They think it means roofing."

"Have you ever seen a shingle beach, Gavin?"

"Never. But I know what they are."

"Ah. They're beautiful with those billions of pebbles but devilish hard to walk on. Now our sand is easier on the feet but it simply wouldn't do in this poem."

Suddenly he made an expansive gesture

155

as he quoted:

> . . . *down the vast edges drear*
> *And naked shingles of the world.*

You see? You couldn't possibly say *sands* there. Shingles is the inevitable word!''

"I agree, and I love the poem. But coming down from the sublime, what are you going to have for your dinner?''

"Oh," Billy said airily, "I don't know. Man does not live by bread alone. You should realize that.''

"That's right. He needs something along with it. Confess. You eat cold cereal three times a day. Right?''

"Well, it's good enough and easy to prepare," Billy defended.

"It's not enough. You must have meat and vegetables. You're pale and you're thin. May I look in your icebox?''

"Sure. You won't find much. That Irish biddy you hired for me cleans it up once a week when she comes, and she manages to cook a little something. Self-preservation, I suppose.''

"I picked up a couple of things as I passed the store and I'd like to cook your dinner tonight. I'm not a bad chef when I set my mind to it."

"Will you stay and eat with me?" His voice had the eagerness of a child.

"Why not?" Gavin said. "I'd like to. I'll call Cecily and tell her I'll be a bit late."

The icebox, as Billy had reported, was practically bare, a little bread and butter and a half bottle of milk. On the shelves, however, were a few cans which Gavin remembered helping Billy to buy once on a shopping trip, and which had evidently been forgotten. Now the mushrooms and tomatoes would help. In the bin were a few sprouting potatoes.

When he was calling Cecily he had a thought. "What's for dessert tonight, darling? Pie? Wonderful. Do you suppose you could send a couple of pieces over here with Ian on his bike?"

While Gavin did the cooking, Billy pushed the books and papers from the table in his living room, rummaged through a drawer of miscellaneous laundry and came up with a somewhat wrinkled but clean white square upon which, when spread, he placed the cutlery. He was nervously delighted, and when they sat down at last to the hamburgers and mushrooms, the vegetables and the rolls Gavin had picked up along the way with the

157

meat and heated, the simple meal evidently took on for Billy the excitement of a feast. He ate prodigiously, casting an eye frequently to where the pie, duly brought by Ian, sat temptingly at the edge of the table.

"It's a good while since you've had dinner with me, Mac," he said.

Gavin, resolving that come what might he would do it more often, replied, "I know, Billy. I seem to get involved with so many things. My trouble is what our friend M. Arnold called 'this strange disease of modern life, with its sick hurry.' Now how the devil did he come to write that nearly a hundred years ago? Looking back at it, it would seem as though his times should have been quite peaceful."

"It's not the *times* that are frenetic," Billy said thoughtfully, "it's the people. They always have been and they always will be, in any age. But now that poem you just quoted from . . ."

They were off. As Gavin had often told Cecily, Billy *when he was sober,* was the most congenial friend in many ways that he had. Sadly enough, this state did not occur too frequently. But he was sober by now, in complete possession of his interesting and well-stocked mind, so the conversation moved from literature to art to philosophy with quick give-and-take. By the time the pie and coffee were finished Billy looked like a new man. There was color in his cheeks and an alertness in his bearing as he expressed his thanks.

"I hate to leave the clearing up to you," Gavin said, "but I'm afraid I'll have to go. I have a lot of work to do. But I want you to make me a promise before I leave."

Billy looked at him warily. "Now, now, Mac, don't spoil things with any preachments. I've told you before . . ."

"Will you hold your horses?" Gavin broke in. "The promise has nothing whatever to do with drinking. What I want is for you to take some money out of your monthly check and buy food with it. Stock up your shelves and your icebox. I'll go with you to shop or I'll go myself if you'd rather. But this *must be done!* No more living on cold cereal. That's out. Will you give me your word?"

"Oh, I guess I can promise that," Billy said, adding slyly, "as long as you don't take too much away from my *real necessities.*"

"O.K. I'll check with you soon. And Billy, I want to tell you how much I've enjoyed this visit with you. It's done me good."

There was a faint mist in Billy's eyes. "Thanks, Mac. That's even better than the dinner."

When Gavin got home he found Cissie asleep, of course, and the boys studying in their rooms. Also that Miss Matthews, suiting her own convenience as usual, had begged Rose and Abe to come back that evening for a special session à deux. She said they had improved so much in the last two weeks she wanted now to bring out any latent talent still untouched.

"I'm quoting," Cecily said. "Rose was very angry. She said tomorrow afternoon would have done just as well only Miss Matthews wanted to leave early then. At any rate Rose kept Abe—and of course Miss Matthews—waiting a long time, during which he visited with me."

She leaned forward in her chair, her hands clasped.

"I don't know, Gavin. I just don't know. I like the boy better each time I'm with him, but whether Rose with her temperament and her *beauty* can ever become reconciled to marrying him . . ."

"Do you think," Gavin asked slowly, "that we should give the whole idea up and pursue another course?"

"But what about Abe? He would be disappointed of his university degree?"

"I'm afraid he stands to be disappointed, no matter which way it goes."

"And there's Aunt Het. No, I think we've gotten into this and will have to go on. If Rose will agree," she added, and a sigh seemed to come from her heart.

"Darling, are you lying awake nights over this? You're pale. I have to look out for you too, you know," Gavin said.

She crossed to him, put her hands on his shoulders and laid her cheek against his. "You can't bear it all. I must carry my half."

He drew her down into his arms. "I am a man," he said. "I took on the responsibilities of a wife and children. I'd be a poor sort if I didn't bear the most of it." Then with a sad smile he added, "But I can't control a heart. Not one as tender as yours. I know that." They sat on, holding each other close for what seemed a long time, then he lifted her gently to the floor.

"Run along to bed now and try to sleep. I have work to do. But I'll bring you up your breakfast in the morning. A good one."

"Oh, just coffee, please Gavin. Then I'll come down later and eat with you and the children. I want terribly to hear how the rehearsal went tonight. You don't mind?"

"Of course I do. I wanted to stagger up the stairs with a bigger tray than usual and have you say, 'Poor, dear Gavin, what a beast of burden he is. But a nice beast withal.' "

They laughed and kissed as he stood beside her for a moment.

"How was Billy?" she asked.

"Sober, by the beard of the prophet, sober! I really enjoyed the visit. We threw poetry back and forth at each other and had a real symposium on art. What a waste that man's life has been, considering his native talents. By the way, while he was eating your pie he said he felt his fears were groundless and that he was in heaven already."

"I must bake him a pie oftener. Do remind me. How was the Judge?"

"Not too bad. I believe we may get him persuaded to go along to the show. But, meanwhile, you go on to bed, my darling."

It was ten the next day when the complete family finally surrounded the breakfast table. There was the usual mixed conversation with Bruce and Ian carrying on most of it. Then at last Cecily said casually, "How did your rehearsal go last night, Rose?"

162

Rose, who had been silent up till now, gave an unexpected little giggle, then turned serious.

"It was pretty awful, but it *did* have its funny side." She looked around as though uncertain how much she should repeat.

"You're in the bosom of your family, Rose," her father said, "and naturally we're all very much interested."

"Well," she began, "you know, I guess, that Miss Matthews is really a slave-driver but she always gets away with it because nobody wants to get thrown out of the Senior play once they're in it. So they just take it as she dishes it out. And she's been roughest on Abe. Of course he *was* pretty awful at first. But now that he's let himself go, he's really not bad and it seems she's quite pleased. But last night," (another small giggle) "she turned all her guns *on me*. I was dead tired, I'll admit, and mad that she made just the two of us go back last night, so after she'd said I was wooden and showed no interest in my acting and my voice was too small for the part anyway, to my horror—if any of you ever tell this," she interpolated, looking at Bruce and Ian, "I'll kill you. Well, I felt the tears running down my cheeks. There I stood crying like a baby.

163

And all at once . . . you'll never believe this . . . Abe simply let fly at her. You never heard such a tongue-lashing as he gave her. And the amazing thing was she *took it!* Never said a word until he stopped for breath, then she came over and patted me and said she realized I'd been working too hard and we'd better go. So we did. But fast.''

"And what did you say when you got in the car?'' Cecily asked breathlessly.

"Well,'' Rose said, "I really was shook up and I couldn't stop crying, and Abe just kept muttering to himself. If it had been anybody else, I'd have thought he was swearing under his breath, but I doubt if Abe knows any cuss words.''

Bruce gave a yelp. "Abe Williams? Why, he drove the mules on their farm before they got the tractor. I would imagine he could use a few expressions not for the record.''

"Oh,'' Rose said indifferently, "I would never have guessed it. He's so . . . so . . . oh, *you* know how he is. When we got back here I thanked him for standing up for me and he just said he didn't think we'd have any more trouble with Miss Matthews, and that was it. But if you could have seen her wilt! And if only the whole cast could have seen her! It really was funny.''

After the general dispersal following breakfast Bruce followed his father up to the study.

''I just thought I'd tell you that your talk with John Partridge did the trick. He's got hold of himself and, by the way, he thinks you're the greatest.''

''But I didn't really talk to him,'' Gavin said uncomfortably.

''You must have, for he told me he looks at things differently now. I . . . I don't want to pry into this but I've been so interested. I just wonder what line you took with him. That is if you care to speak of it.''

Gavin looked embarrassed. ''I don't mind, but there's so little to tell. John had the idea that every man around his father's age or before either went after another woman as his father had, or wanted to. I just told him that wasn't the way with me, and he thanked me and went out! That was all there was to it.''

''I guess,'' Bruce replied slowly, ''that must have been enough.'' Then he added, ''I can tell you, Pop, it gives a guy a pretty comfortable feeling to know the sky isn't just suddenly going to fall on his head. You might tell Mother that sometime, for I'd be sure to get sloppy if I tried to. Well, thanks anyway. For *everything.*" With a breezy gesture Bruce had gone.

But Gavin sat down at his desk, a dimness in his eyes. *Many a green isle needs must be,* he murmured to himself. "And I've just seen one of them."

As the week of the play approached it was evident that Rose was nervous. Her parents imputed it to the demands of the role itself, but on a night that they were alone in the living room she came in and began, with a set face, to speak to them.

"I *can't* go on any longer without knowing what you are planning for me. I've tried so hard to do as you asked. I've kept my mind fixed on my college work and the play. I've never given away my secret even to Sara Lee who's been my best friend as you know since we were in kindergarten. I've tried to follow all your suggestions and ask no questions but the weeks are passing and I feel I *must* know what is in your minds!"

"I don't wonder, dear child, that you are confused or even impatient," Cecily said. "But I hardly need tell you that your father and I have not have been idle in our planning for you. Could you wait another week? Just until after the play, and then we will tell you what we've been thinking of, and you can decide."

Rose drew a quivering breath "Of course I can wait that much longer. It's just that sometimes I panic and more so when I feel completely in the dark. But thanks so terribly for all you are doing. I just hope I can go along with your idea, whatever it is."

When she had gone out Gavin spoke, heavily, "I'm going to have another talk with the boy," he said. "There are some things that have to be said. For Rose's sake."

The opportunity came easily the next afternoon. Gavin was driving home, and after the last period he said casually to Abe, "Can I give you a lift? We can chat a little on the way."

"Of course," the boy said promptly. "Thanks. That will be a big help, for we rehearse again tonight."

They were quiet until they were out in the country with snowy drifts of dogwood bordering the road, and in the fields the young green wheat and fresh brown furrows from the early ploughing.

Gavin cleared his throat and began. "There's something on my mind, Abe, and I don't know just how to say it. If Rose agrees to marry you, there is her condition increasingly to consider and the fact that she doesn't love you; and I felt on top of everything else you might have to use a good deal of courtesy and forbearance . . . oh, I'm not sure you understand what I'm talking about."

Abe's reply was serious and yet there was what might be termed a half-smile within it.

"I'm not a child, Mr. McAllister. I know perfectly well what you're talking about. I've given a lot of thought to it myself. I love Rose, which will make it all harder yet in a way easier, for you see I want to take care of her. And if she will go through a marriage ceremony with me, you can be dead sure I'll never presume on that for more than it's worth in this case. From the letter you showed me there are two rooms upstairs. I'll be working like the very devil as soon as I get into the university and I'll never bother her. But I'll be there, Mr. McAllister. I'll be *there* whenever she needs me."

Gavin reached over and touched the boy's hand. His voice was unsteady.

"However this whole thing turns out, Abe, I'll always feel you're like a son to me."

"That's the most wonderful thing you could say," Abe answered, his own voice husky. "I only hope I'll be worth it."

There was another matter to be settled, and upon this they were not at first in accord. Abe had assumed the plan would be broached to Rose by her parents. And indeed Gavin had at first thought the same thing. But after deep consideration he and Cecily had decided this would be a mistake. For one thing it would make it a purely mechanical arrangement, leaving out entirely the fact of Abe's love. It was due him, they thought, that he should confess his own feelings (which in this case included complete knowledge of the facts) and beg Rose to marry him as any man would ask a girl. In the second place by this method Rose might feel her sorely wounded pride was somewhat assuaged.

When Gavin now presented these views to Abe, the latter repudiated them almost with violence. If her parents told her the whole plan, he said, she would have time at least to get over the shock and think about it. If Abe blurted it all out (his words) himself, she would refuse at that very moment. She didn't like him. She had been a little nicer to him of late, but it was only on account of the play. Besides, if he tried to tell her all he would like to say, he would stammer and muddle everything up. No, the McAllisters would have to break it all to her, if there was to be any chance of success.

They talked on and on, the spring air enfolding them as though the sharp outlines of the day and of their own problems were subdued by its gentle compassion.

Abe argued well, but Gavin argued better. At the end the boy drew a long sigh. "I'll try it," he said, "if you really think it's best, but I'm afraid I'll ruin everything. I won't know what to say."

"You're a young man in love," Gavin said, "and I've found you very articulate. Just tell her what you feel and you can't go wrong. Also you might mention, if you can, what we talked about first tonight—Aunt Het's two bedrooms on the second floor and all that. It just might have some bearing on the case."

"Oh sure! I'll make all that clear enough."

"Our conversation won't throw you off for your show, will it, Abe? I'm afraid I never thought about that."

"No. Just the opposite. You see I've been puzzling over a lot of things, and now I feel better since we've brought them all out in the open and I have your advice."

"I hear Miss Matthews is eating out of your hand now," Gavin laughed.

Abe flushed. "I don't know yet how I ever got the nerve to fly out at her. I've taken enough from her, God knows, and I still would have but when she turned nasty to Rose, I just sort of saw red, I guess."

"Good for you!" Gavin said heartily. "I hope I haven't kept you too late tonight."

They parted with a warm handshake and Gavin drove home, a relieved, almost secure feeling in his heart. *I would ask nothing better for my daughter,* he was thinking, *than that boy with the rough edges rubbed off him.* Who ever said that miracles never happened now? Silly fools! They were always happening one way or another. Why not believe in them?

The next afternoon a note was brought to Gavin's desk. It stated tersely that his presence was desired in Dr. Waring's office at the end of the last period.

Now, what's up? he wondered. More discussion about Commencement, he supposed. But as he ran into Devereux in the hall later, he was puzzled.

"Going up to faculty meeting?" he asked.

"Didn't know there was one."

When Gavin showed his slip of paper, Devereux looked worried.

"Gavin, for the love of the Lord, be nice to him. It pays sometimes to turn the other cheek."

"Why wouldn't I be nice to him? I don't know what he wants, but I doubt if it's anything serious. Just some picayune thing probably. I'll let you know."

And Gavin went on up the stairs and finally entered the President's private office.

"Good afternoon, Dr. Waring. You wished to see me?" His tone was cordial and confident.

The Doctor seemed a trifle less so. "Ah, yes, yes, Professor McAllister. Very good of you to drop in. I do have a matter I want to talk over with you. Of a somewhat unfortunate nature, I fear."

"Unfortunate?"

"Perhaps rather, in a sense, unpleasant would be a more accurate term."

Gavin sat very still, waiting, his heart giving fast premonitory beats.

"Not to prolong it, the point is simply this. We are very anxious to raise the academic standard of Marsden. You are doubtless aware that of all the heads of departments you are the only one who does not have a Doctorate. The trustees feel that in spite of the quality of your teaching,

172

which is, we know, high, the head of the English department, perhaps the most important one in the college, should be a Professor with a Doctor's degree. And so . . ."

Gavin's voice was pure ice. "And so?"

Dr. Waring looked definitely uncomfortable. "And so we are now in the process of trying to locate a new teacher with the desired degree for the head of the English department. I felt it was only fair to apprise you of our intention now, though we hope you will remain with us and continue the fine work you have always done."

"But under this new man?"

"Well, yes, of necessity that would be so. Just as, by the same token, he would naturally take over the Senior English classes."

Gavin slowly drew a sheet of paper from his briefcase and a pen from his pocket. As the President watched him, fascinated, he wrote upon the paper, rose and laid it on Dr. Waring's desk.

"That," he said, "is my resignation, to take effect the last day of this term. I will not teach here another year under the arrangement you mention. That to me is definitely *infra dig,* if you are familiar with the expression. The quality of my teaching is above that and I resent having such a proposition made to me. You will have no trouble in finding the sort of man you are looking for. Degrees in themselves are a dime a dozen. Good teachers are not. I wish you success in your search."

He turned to go, his face stone white. Dr. Waring came sputtering after him. "But my dear Mr. McAllister, you can't leave us like this. The work you have done here is highly respected and you have many friends. We simply want all our departments to be on an academic level. Perhaps when you think it over . . ."

"My resignation is before you. No amount of time and thought can change my decision. And I would like to add this."

He turned sharply and faced Dr. Waring who now looked somewhat dismayed. He had evidently run his hand in an unaccustomed gesture through his hair and the long side fringe which ordinarily was carefully brushed over the bald spot was now falling here and there in disarrangement.

"I can now say this to you since I'm leaving. I know exactly why you wanted to fire me—which is what it amounts to. You are doing it out of spite. Out of a desire to get even with me for what I said at the faculty meeting when you suggested we should all do an unethical, a dishonest thing. Well, you have achieved your end."

He went out of the room with Dr. Waring's voice vacantly following him. He went down the stairs for the first time holding on to the railing. On the first floor he went to the telephone in the hall and called Cecily.

"Listen, darling, I may be a little late so don't wait dinner for me, and don't worry about me."

"Aren't you well?" As always she knew from his voice that something was wrong.

"Perfectly. It's just that once in a while I need to get off by myself and think when things crowd in on me. You understand?"

"Of course. I'll save some dinner for you. You're sure you're all right?"

"I will be when I see you."

He drove through the hilly, winding streets of the town, out the main road, and still on until his eyes could see the far rolling lines of the Blue Ridge. Here he ran the car into a deserted lane and sank back, shaking as if from a chill. He felt an utter desolation, a despair creep over him. With a few strokes of his pen he had thrown away next year's sustenance for his family. How had he dared to do such a thing? And yet, he knew he could have done no other. With the realization of his own capabilities there went a pride, partly born of this knowledge and partly of his racial inheritance. The blood of those who had fought at Bannockburn flowed in his own veins. Well, in any case, the thing was done.

He went over carefully in his mind the politics involved in his ultimate dismissal. Waring would have initiated it. Of this he was sure. But one trustee would at once have gone along with him. This was Loren Scott. Gavin remembered that the day when he had all but choked the breath out of the man he had said, "I'll never mention this to anyone because of the circumstances, but *I won't forget it.*" The other trustees, a number of them Gavin's friends, would finally be persuaded. So, it had been worked. The one thing they had not counted upon was his immediate resignation. There might even be some criticism of the methods used. However, Waring had a genius for mollification. His tact, his suavity, his ability when necessary to make two and two equal five, had kept the trustees satisfied and even more important, kept the alumni content in the belief that the College was in the best possible hands and thus willing to donate more and more for its support. Indeed, Waring had certain native gifts which more brilliant and distinguished Presidents might have envied.

But this mental debt having been paid, Gavin crouched lower in his car while convulsive waves of anger swept over him. What was he going to *do?* He must find a job near enough so that Bruce could complete his Senior year. And for himself to go with his hat in his hand to interview new trustees and school directors, and finally take—if he could get it—an inferior position, this would be humiliating to his very soul. And all because of the machinations of one little, spiteful, and, he felt, fundamentally dishonest man!

He raised himself and gripped the wheel as though to wrench it from its base. "I loathe him!" he said aloud. Then he shouted it. "I despise him! I hate him! *I hate him!*"

Then slowly at long last he loosed his hold and bent his head upon the wheel. Tears are not easy to a man; they are like blood-drops from his heart. But Gavin wept now as the words, in his weakness and his wretchedness, were wrung from him.

"What price *empathy*," he said.

Five

ONE THING GAVIN decided as he drove back slowly through the gathering dusk. This was that he would not share the secret with Cecily. At least, not yet. It would be the first time in their married lives that he had withheld from her information vital to them both, but he could not lay upon her heart now one more burden. The next night was the play. After that Rose would know the truth about their plan and what would happen then no one could foretell. As to his own problem he must begin to take action soon for there was not much time. His best confidant would be Bob St. Clair as soon as this perilous weekend was over.

When he reached home he found the house quiet and Cecily sitting at the piano with an old music score propped up in front of her. She was running through snatches of *The Student Prince.* At the sound of his step she got up at once, her face anxious.

"Oh Gavin, I've been so worried about you. Whatever kept you so late?"

He forced a feeble grin. "Have you sought sanctuary in your room occasionally to weep a little weep when you didn't want anyone, even me, to come near you?"

"Perhaps," she admitted, "but certainly not often."

"Well, that was the general feeling I had, translated into masculine terms, so I drove out into a country lane and fought all my 'scares' out with myself. Do you want to know my present state?"

"I certainly do."

"I'm hungry. I'm ravenous."

"Oh, I couldn't be happier than to hear that. We had a good dinner but I was so worried about you I couldn't eat. I'll go now and heat up the leftovers and then I'll dine with you."

"Wasn't that the show music you were playing?" he asked as they sat down at the table.

"As well as I could manage it. It's strange that during these last weeks I haven't gone over it before. Of course Rose has been working from a cut score. And I hope it's been cut enough. I had forgotten how difficult it is. Rose said, you know, that Miss Matthews picked the best voices in college amongst both the girls and the boys to keep any of the songs from sounding too thin, and also of course to give the chance for a large cast. It's just possible that, slave-driver or not, Miss Matthews knows what she's doing."

"We'll find out tomorrow night. If the old adage holds, tonight's dress rehearsal will be a flop."

"I don't believe that. They'll all do better, of course, at the real performance, but I have a feeling tonight won't be too bad. They're well trained. Should we wait for Rose?"

"I don't believe so. In the first place I don't think I could hold up and also since we *must* wait up tomorrow after the show . . . ."

"Yes. Tonight would be a little too much. Can you imagine *living* after this weekend is over?"

"Oh, yes. It just could be we'll feel better."

"Gavin, this afternoon Sara Lee came in to visit with Rose. I was in the sewing room so I couldn't help but overhear. The chief topic was the Prom."

"How did she say it went?"

"Great success. She said the music was divine. Plenty of rock and roll and brass, and then it seems the waltz at the end was a hit."

"Good!"

"She said everyone groaned a little when it was announced but when they got in the swing of it, it was positively *dreamy,* I quote. But she pressed Rose unmercifully as to why she hadn't gone. Rose held out very well. Said she was too dead tired from rehearsals and also that she had no date. Sara Lee just made a joke of that. 'Not even Honest Abe?' 'Not even anybody,' Rose answered. And then . . . I thought this was pitiful, Gavin."

"Tell me."

"Sara Lee asked if Rose would have gone to the Prom if she'd still been dating Lester Scott seriously."

"What did she say?" His voice was tense.

"She said she probably would." Cecily drew a long sigh. "Sara Lee told her she was well out of that. That a good many girls wouldn't date him now for fear they'd get their necks broken. It seems the last time he was picked up he was doing ninety and one more ticket will stop everything, license, car and all. She says he's going to France right after Commencement and someone ought to warn them what was coming. That was about all, but there is a sad little note there, isn't there, Gavin?"

"Bound to be, I guess."

They were in bed when Rose returned but found a note in the kitchen the next morning.

Rugged night but rehearsal not too bad. Think I'll sleep in tomorrow.

ROSE

The hours of the new day, the fateful day, passed in their punctual round. No one watching Cecily and Gavin could have guessed their accelerated heart beats. As a sort of background drum to all their actions were the constant words: *Tonight we'll know. We'll know.*

Cecily prepared an early dinner. It had been decided to take little Cissie along as a great treat so the child's excited comments helped to relieve the strain. Rose had to be at the college by seven, and they saw her off with good wishes, as casual as they could manage.

"I'll run you over," Gavin had said as she finished her dinner.

"Oh, Abe's picking me up. He has to be

there at the same time."

Cecily kissed her tenderly. "You look beautiful, dear, and you're in such good voice you couldn't possibly be nervous. We can't wait to hear you. And the whole cast," she added.

Rose thanked them and left as a step was heard on the porch.

"It's odd he didn't come in," Cecily said.

"Oh, the boy has plenty on his mind tonight," Gavin answered.

Bob St. Clair had insisted upon driving the family over. "You're too excited to know where you're going, Gavin," he argued. So at seven-thirty he arrived in his big car to collect Cecily and Gavin and little Cissie, and a bit later the Judge, in his best blacks.

When they reached the campus they found the parking space already limited and, once in the auditorium at a quarter to eight, practically every seat already filled.

"What a crowd!" Bob exclaimed. "This had better be good."

The last comers were barely in their places when the orchestra began the overture and in a short time the curtain went up to delighted hand-clapping. The scenery, built by the boys in the wood-working department, painted by Miss Carney and her students in art, and furbished and decorated by the girls of the cast, was a triumph! Before the eyes of the audience was spread, vividly, the courtyard and inn at Old Heidelberg. The bright costumes and gay opening songs sent murmurs of approval from row to row.

"Good Lord," Bob whispered to Gavin, "I never expected anything like this. They're almost professional."

"Pretty good," Gavin answered with becoming restraint. As a matter of fact he was listening intently and with the faintest shade of disappointment for Abe's voice, as he had imagined it. Rose was at her best as she soared above the choruses and in her brief solos, and Abe was good, *very* good, but . . .

It was at the beginning of the second act that it happened. The orchestra swung into the first strains of the famous "Serenade." Abe stood looking up toward the little inn window where Rose's face could be seen. For a line or two he sang almost softly, then suddenly there was a change. Generations of Welshmen, singing in their homes, in their churches, singing as they walked over the cobblestones on their way to the mines—all of this was in Abe's blood, all of this was in his rich baritone which, rising at last to its full power, swept the audience with it like a wave of the sea.

Overhead the moon is beaming,
White as blossoms on the bough;
Nothing is heard but the song of a bird,
Filling all the air with dreaming!
Could my heart but still its beating,
Only you can tell it how!
Beloved!
From your window give me greeting,
Hear my eternal vow!
. . . . .
Soft in the trees, sighs the echo of my
    longing,
While all around you my dreams of
    rapture throng.

Here the muted strings alone seemed to increase the hush that had fallen upon the audience, then the voice again, in all its strength.

My soul, my joy—my hope, my fear,
Your heart must tell you that I am near.
Lean from above, while I pour out my
    love,
For you know to my life you are love!
Oh, hear my longing cry!

Oh, love me or I die!

. . . . .

From your window give me greeting.
I swear my eternal love!

At the end there was a second of continued
hush, and then came the applause. But it was
not merely applause, it was thunder. The
room seemed to shake with it. Abe stood,
flushed both with embarrassment and
pleasure, not quite certain what to do next as
the applause continued unabated. It was
evident that neither he nor Miss Matthews
had expected anything like this. The orchestra
leader settled it by raising his baton and
nodding to Abe. There was absolute quiet as
the melody rose on the air, and then, again,
Abe's voice. Perhaps because of the ovation
or perhaps due to some great release within
himself, Abe poured forth his heart with
startling intensity. He was all lover. Only
three people in the audience knew the truth,
but a subtle transference seemed somehow to
pass from singer to listeners. It could be felt
almost as a tangible thing through the
emotional breathing of a thousand people.

Oh, hear my longing cry!
Oh, love me or I die!

. . . . .
All my heart for you is beating,
Only you can tell it how!
Beloved!
From your window give me greeting,
Hear my eternal vow!

The applause once more was deafening,
but the orchestra moved at once into the next
song and Abe, with a stiff little inclination of
his head, retired to his next position on the
stage.

The rest of the play was excellent—gay,
tender or moving, according to the demands
of the plot—with Rose's voice more clear
and pure with each of her numbers.
However, no one could help but feel that the
biggest moment had been passed and that it
was Abe Williams who had "stopped the
show."

At the end there were many curtain calls,
Miss Matthews seeing to it that the cast was
properly applauded, while she, herself,
propelled by the happy young Thespians,
took a well-deserved bow. Then small groups
of the leading actors by threes and fours
came forward to receive their ovations, until
at the last Abe and Rose alone came to stand
in front of the footlights. Someone started it,

and in a minute of time the whole audience was on its feet, while the clapping continued. From the back of the room where the college students had been sitting came shouts of "Encore! Encore! Give us 'The Serenade,' Abe!"

Abe leaned towards the conductor and the melody began again. He sang only the first few lines but as he did, quite unconsciously, it seemed, he reached for Rose's hand. Then the curtain came down with definite finality. The play was over.

The Judge was mopping the tears from his cheeks while Cecily and many other women were wiping their eyes.

"By George," Bob kept saying, "I haven't heard anything as good as that in a long time. Who's the boy?"

"Abe Williams."

"Live here in Marsden?"

"Out in the country. You met him at our house one night. Don't you remember?"

"No! It can't be the same? Not that embarrassed kid? Why, in this uniform he looks positively handsome. Going in for a musical career, I suppose?"

"I don't think so," Gavin answered briefly. "That's a hard row to hoe."

"With that voice?"

Cecily broke in. "There will be such a mob backstage and we're sure to see Rose and Abe later, don't you think we'd better just go on? We can congratulate Miss Matthews another time."

On the way back, the conversation of course still centered on the play, the Judge and Bob both being eloquent in their amazement and praise. For the most part Gavin and Cecily allowed the talk to ebb and flow around them, saying little. Bob kept glancing at them keenly. When they had dropped the Judge off and had reached the McAllisters' he said, "I don't believe I'll come in, Cecily. From the looks of you two, you're pretty well bushed and no wonder. It must have been quite a strain waiting for this thing to come off. Well, you can relax now. It was a hit from the first line. Rose was divine and that young Abe—did you say his name was?—certainly brought down the house. I'll be seeing you soon."

After the good-byes, Gavin and Cecily came into the living room and looked at each other.

"We have no idea when they'll get here," Gavin said, "especially if they go to the party."

"Rose thought they would probably come

190

straight home."

"Good idea, except that they both deserve the plaudits of their peers." He drew a long sigh and began pacing the floor. "Have you ever seen a Marsden audience rise to its feet as it did tonight?"

"Never."

"Nor have I. We have just witnessed a rather remarkable performance."

"I'll make some coffee," she said. "That may help us while we're waiting."

Gavin continued pacing the floor, the coffee cup in his hand, while Cecily leaned back on the sofa exhausted. It was after one when they heard the car and both grew tense, listening. But there were no voices to accompany the footsteps on the walk and only a low word or two at the door as Rose opened it and came in, alone.

"Oh, my dear," her mother exclaimed, "where's Abe?"

"Going home, I guess."

"But the *play,* Rose, you were wonderful and Abe really past belief. Daddy and I were just saying . . ."

"I don't want to talk about the play. I want to talk about *me*. Abe told me on the way home what you've done. Telling him everything, practically offering me for sale as

191

though I had no shame, no pride, and to Abe Williams of all people. Oh, how could you do this to me? How *could* you?''

Gavin's voice was husky. "Did Abe tell you he was in love with you, had been for a long time?''

"Oh yes, he *would* say that in the spot you've put him in. Even if that were true it certainly doesn't follow that I love him.''

"Did he,'' Gavin went on, "explain that if you were married he would not be in any way . . . demanding . . .''

"Oh, yes, he blundered around about that. But Daddy that would be an impossible situation. Suppose we married and I never . . . slept with him. What would *he* get out of it all? Going way over there to hunt a job in a strange city . . .''

"He didn't tell you he intends if he is there to study for his Master's at the University of Edinburgh?''

"He . . . *what?* Why that's ridiculous. His family are just struggling along to buy that little farm. Where on earth would Abe get the money to do that?''

"I have a little put aside I meant to use for that purpose,'' Gavin said quietly.

Rose's face turned white. She looked at her father, then at her mother, and back again to him.

"Will you tell me the truth? Is this the money that you've been saving for so long to allow you to take a year off to get your own Doctorate? Is it, Mother?" she persisted when Gavin didn't speak.

"Yes, dear, it is," her mother said.

Rose stood up, still looking from one to the other. In spite of her pallor her parents thought she had never looked so beautiful. She crossed the room to her father.

"Daddy, do you really mean you would do this for me? Make this sacrifice?"

"It's nothing," Gavin protested, almost harshly in the intensity of his feeling. "What else could possibly matter as much as you?"

She laid her head for a moment upon his breast, then raised her eyes to his. He could feel her trembling and put his arms about her.

"I'll marry Abe whenever you say. And I believe it should be as soon as possible. The minute Commencement is over. I'll go on up now."

Her father still kept her within his arm. "Dear child," he said, "Abe has had no chance to enjoy his great success tonight. I think he's probably very unhappy now, for I happen to know that he really loves you. I'm going to call him up to congratulate him on his singing. Would you be willing to add a word telling him you are going to accept his proposal?"

Rose sighed heavily. "I suppose one time is as good as another."

When someone answered the phone, it proved to be Abe's young brother. "I don't know whether he's here or not but I'll look around." In a minute he was back. "He's been sitting out in the car all by himself but he's coming in now."

Gavin tried to make his voice natural. "Abe? I can't tell you how proud we are of you. You gave a simply marvelous performance. And here is Rose to speak to you."

Rose swallowed painfully. "Abe?" There was a low voice at the other end of the wire. "I was pretty much s-startled you know by our talk as we were driving home but I've been thinking it all over and I am going to agree to the plan."

Gavin could not hear Abe's words but Rose answered them at once.

"Of my own free will, *of course*. How could you think otherwise? I can't see you tomorrow for I'm going to sleep all day but after that we can . . . . discuss things. Goodnight."

Gavin drew her closer. "That was a better performance than you gave in the play, and we were proud enough of you, dear, in that. Now up to bed with you. You've crossed the first hurdle already."

By the beginning of the week Rose looked rested and her color had come back. She was very quiet, however, and when possible avoided answering the phone calls, of which there were many. Abe had come in Sunday evening and they had gone for a drive, a long one apparently, or, Gavin thought, perhaps just as far as a quiet parking spot, such as he himself had found. It was Rose later who told them gently but firmly, as though she were speaking to children, the arrangements she and Abe had decided upon.

"I hope you will not be too hurt by this, but I simply can't have anything that seems like a . . . a . . . wedding, even with only the family here at home. The point is, if you were present at all I'd go to pieces. I couldn't hold up. So Abe suggested we just go to the church before we leave that . . . that night. He will speak to Dr. Stevens, and of course attend to the license and we'll go to the new young doctor for our blood tests. Dr. Stevens could probably get his wife and her sister just to slip in for witnesses. We'll take the ten-four for New York right after. Oh," she burst out, "I hope you won't be hurt but if I do it at all, this is the only way."

"And very sensible, Rose," Gavin said calmly, seeing Cecily's stricken face. "You can leave here without any fuss, making it easier for us too."

"Oh, you really feel like that?" Her voice was choked with relief.

"Certainly. Your judgment and Abe's is sure to be better than ours about this."

"If we l-leave the Monday night of Commencement day, we could get our plane on Tuesday morning."

"Very good. I'll send a cable to Aunt Het at once, and check about your flight."

"I'm so glad," Rose added, "that you've taken this as you have."

That last week it seemed to Gavin that Cecily's eyes were never dry except when she assumed a forced brightness at meal times. She, of course, had the hardest part, sorting and packing Rose's clothes, considering, deciding, sometimes holding a filmy bit of negligee to her lips, to her heart. She added a new quilted satin robe for warmth in the Scottish nights. She bought a little blue hat faced with white which would go with the last year's suit now freshly cleaned and pressed. She racked her brain to remember small things that might bring just enough without too much thought of home. At the very last she wrote a long letter filled with love, and encouragement, and all sorts of practical advice drawn from her own experience, and laid it underneath the garments.

Gavin had called the boys into his study one evening and told them of the coming marriage. Later he would probably tell them all. Just now perhaps the simple fact was best.

"And it has all come so suddenly, that Rose is quite emotionally upset about going so far away, so she doesn't want any of us to be at the ceremony. They'll just go quietly to the church Monday evening and then take the night train for New York, and the plane next day. So I think the best thing would be to treat it lightly, kid her along a little, but tell her how much you'll miss her. You'll know what to do, but have some pressing engagements that night after dinner so you won't be here when she leaves. O.K.?"

Bruce's eyes looked keenly at his father. "Wasn't this pretty quick work?" he said.

Gavin did not face him. "Oh, well, you know these things often strike with lightning rapidity. The play was . . .''

"Gosh, yes," Ian put in, "they certainly looked goners all right on the stage. But gee, we'll miss Rose."

"We sure will," Bruce said heavily.

Gavin watched the boys with something like admiration during the next days; Bruce especially, whom he suspected of knowing the whole story, had the lightest touch.

"Well, Rosie," he began, knowing she disliked the name, "if you haven't pulled a fast one! What's the idea of keeping us in the dark until now? We're your loving brothers, don't you remember? But all kidding aside, Rose, you couldn't have picked a nicer guy. I'll be very pleased to have Abe as a brother-in-law."

As the week passed Gavin talked with Abe in the evenings, explained what he had done about money matters, also that he had made Pullman reservations for the night they left, and gotten plane seats for the following day. He made small but important suggestions to the boy about matters he had probably never thought of. Gavin, too, was racking his brain, even as Cecily, to forget nothing for their child's comfort.

The week moved in its time-honored Marsden course. The last exams came and went, the Baccalaureate sermon was duly preached, the day of Commencement itself, toward which four years had moved, arrived with a burst of June sunshine and roses. At ten-thirty the academic procession formed in Main Hall to lead the way into the auditorium. Gavin was acutely conscious of his Master's hood, amongst the reds of the Doctorates. Devereux sidled up to him.

"Look," he said, "where have you been hiding lately? 'Those friends thou hast, should oft be seen,' etc. What did the big white Papa want with you last week?"

"I'll tell you later. In fact I very much want to talk to you."

"As bad as that?"

"Well bad enough. You've got E.S.P. Say, we'd better get in line."

The graduates advanced two by two to the strains of "Pomp and Circumstance." Gavin, now on the platform, saw only three clearly: Rose with a fixed expression on her flushed face, Abe with a look of strain as though he might not have slept the night before, and Lester Scott with his gay, debonair smile and slight swagger.

There was the usual careful division of devotional duties amongst the town's clergy; there was the address itself, impossibly dull

Gavin thought; there was Dr. Waring's spread-eagle announcement of the gift for the new library, received with tumultuous acclaim; there was the awarding of the diplomas with Dr. Waring's introduction and general blessing upon those who were now "leaving the shelter of these cherished halls to go out into the world at large to engage upon their various careers, bravely greeting the future, while remembering the past."

It was done. Clutching the small leather folders containing the precious papers, the graduates rose with a scraping of chairs on the platform, the audience standing also for the singing of the Marsden College song, and then the final benediction.

The new plans for the alumni reception and luncheon were being carried out and the black caps and gowns were now dispersed over the greensward amongst much laughter and excited calling as the fresh alumni made their way toward the other building.

"I think we're supposed to go to this damned thing," Devereux said as he caught up with Gavin. "I had hoped maybe we could all sit together, somewhere near a door so we could slip out if the air got too heavy with Auld Lang Syne. But it seems we not only have to grace the reception but the luncheon table as well. 'So far does Dr. Waring spread his claws. . . .' Listen, I've never had a chance to talk over the play with you. You've always slipped through my fingers. It was really a triumph. And do you know what Marie says? She vows that if Abe isn't in love with Rose this very minute she never saw the Eiffel Tower. How about it?"

"Now, now, you ought to have more sense than to ask a mere father about his daughter's love affairs. And, you know, Devereux, I think Cecily and I will just slip away now, Dr. Waring to the contrary. If anyone asks, just say Cecily had a dreadful headache. Convenient and in this case correct. And I really do want to see you soon."

That evening Cecily held dinner back as long as she could so the interval before leaving would be shorter, for the tension was hard to bear. Rose appeared at the table in an old negligee she was not taking with her, but it was evident the food she ate was forced down with difficulty. The boys kept up a running fire of light conversation. Little Cissie by prearrangement was staying overnight with one of her friends, for Rose had always been utterly devoted to the child and Cecily felt a farewell to her would be the last unendurable heartache.

When dessert was over Bruce and Ian asked to be excused and made ready to leave.

"I'm awfully sorry to be barging off so soon, Rose, but we've both got dates and Dad is letting us have the car," Bruce began. "The very best to you and Abe. You're a lucky pair to have a winter in Edinburgh and you'll be back before we know it. I've just been horsing around a lot but you know we'll miss you like . . . like hell." He gave her a kiss and made hastily for the door.

"That goes for me, too," Ian said, following his brother's example.

Rose put her head in her hands for a long minute and then, without speaking, started up the stairs. She was ready when Abe arrived bearing a square white box. He handed it to her, smiling, but as she fumbled with the string he untied it, opened the lid and drew out a cluster of gardenias, which Gavin had suggested.

"Thanks, Abe," she said huskily. "They're lovely." But her hand was unsteady as she tried to fasten them to her lapel, so his strong fingers attached them.

Abe shook hands with Gavin in good-bye, finding speech impossible, and with Cecily who reached up and kissed him. Then Rose clung to her father, who murmured reassuring words. "My dear child, you're going to love Aunt Het, and Edinburgh itself. There will be so much to interest you. We'll write very often and tell you all the news. God bless you both, my dear."

But when Rose come to her mother she flung herself, sobbing into her arms. "Mother, I can't do it. Oh, I *can't! I'm so scared.*"

In the terrible moment's hush when Gavin and Cecily stood paralyzed in their anguish it was the boy who took charge. He drew Rose's arm through his own.

"Come on, Rose," he said gently, "there's nothing to be afraid of. Everything's going to be all right."

He quietly guided her toward the door. Once there he glanced at the man and woman behind them. But Rose did not look back.

If one listened carefully, one could hear the Main Line trains from the McAllister house. This night, lying in bed exhausted, Gavin and Cecily heard faintly the great 10:04 as it set off for its long pull over the mountains. At first Cecily had trembled at the sound, with all it suggested. "I can't bear it!" she said brokenly.

"It's out of our hands now, darling, and I think well out of them. Try to relax and go to sleep. There is nothing more now we can do."

Before long he could tell by her breathing that she had done so. But he could not. He lay, tense and alert, thinking of the darkened coach and the two young, troubled hearts being borne swiftly along in their strange surroundings to their still stranger ultimate destination. In his own body he could feel the great engine gathering power for its climb. It would now be past Johnstown with the mountains facing it. Up . . . up . . . up, creaking, swaying, shuddering over its ties, until the summit was reached at last. Gallitzin, Cresson, and then, Altoona. As though panting from its effort the black monster would lie for a while at Harrisburg, before moving quietly on through the fair and level country beyond. Lancaster, Paoli, Philadelphia and at the last—New York.

"I have traversed every mile of the way with them this night," Gavin whispered to himself.

It was bright morning and New York would already have been reached before he, too, fell asleep.

When Gavin rose from his brief slumbers, Cecily was getting breakfast and the sharp smell of coffee helped to rouse his numbed brain. He had felt he must wait until today to take his first steps toward finding a new job and had decided to see Bob St. Clair who always seemed to know somebody who in turn knew somebody else. He made excuse of errands and set off as soon as he could. Cecily, he noted, looked better than for some days. It would be easier for both of them to relax now.

He found Bob busy, as usual, but ready to push back his papers and listen when he had looked keenly at Gavin's face.

"I wouldn't have come at this hour, Bob, but I want your help in a sort of double emergency. Here is the first," he said, as he pushed a typewritten page across the desk. "Could you get this in the evening paper? Read it aloud so I'll know how it sounds."

Bob read slowly, his face showing something like consternation as he did so.

"Mr. and Mrs. Gavin McAllister announce the marriage of their daughter, Cecily Rose, to Mr. Abraham Williams, son of Mr. and Mrs. Richard Williams, on

Monday evening in the Presbyterian Church, the Reverend Dr. Stevens officiating.

The young couple left immediately after for New York whence they will emplane Tuesday for Scotland where Mr. Williams plans to pursue his studies at the University of Edinburgh. While there, they will reside with Mrs. Williams' great-aunt, Miss Hettie McAllister.

The best wishes of their many friends go with the young people, who are both this year's Marsden graduates and who also took the leads with distinction in the recent College play.''

Bob read it over again to himself and then looked keenly at Gavin. ''I don't want to be inquisitive, but it strikes me there is more to this than meets the eye. I was worried about Rose's reaction that evening I was at your house. How about it?''

''You are my friend?''

Bob smiled. ''I've thought so, at times.''

''Then this is all you know. The young people were thrown constantly together practicing for the play. They fell in love, were married at once because of Abe's plans for study abroad. Neither of them wanted a big wedding. This was more romantic, don't you see? So, that's your story."

"And I'll stick to it and send them my blessing. Now for the paper." He rang up *The Star* and got the managing editor. A boy would come up at once for the copy. So that was taken care of.

"Now what's your other emergency? It will have to be a big one to top this."

"It is," Gavin said. "I've been fired from my job."

"You what?"

"It's true. At least my resignation was made inevitable. I had a run-in with Waring over a matter some time ago. He asked the faculty to do something I felt was not ethical and I said so I suppose too strongly. Anyway, he never forgot it. The pretext now is that I'm the only head of a department there who doesn't have a Doctorate. He said they were trying to locate a man with the degree and I would be teaching under him, giving up my Senior classes, and I promptly resigned. Maybe I was too hasty, but the more I think of what he said, the more I feel I could have done nothing else. Now, the problem is, where do I find another position? Have you any possible ideas?"

Bob leaned forward, his chin in his hands.

"This is a beaut, all right, Gavin, this that you've come up with. But knowing you as I do, I would be willing to swear you'd done the right thing. As to the new job, that's something else again. Must it be near? You want to stay on in your home at present if you can?"

Gavin drew a deep breath. "Yes, of course, chiefly for Cecily's sake. She loves it. But there is Bruce to consider. He's a Senior next year. I must see him through that if it's humanly possible. But I've racked my brain and all I come up with is St. Dominic's over the hill. Do you suppose I'd have a chance?"

Bob shook his head. "I ought to be able to help you with that for I do their law work, but the trouble is Father Paul runs a tight little ship, mostly Jesuit. I doubt if he would look on you with favor, Gavin. The only place I really could put in an oar for you is the High School. Would you consider such an opening if it came about?"

Gavin's face was a study. He did not answer for a moment and then he said slowly, "I might have to."

"I know Hastings, the principal, pretty well. Good man. I think if anything came of this you two would hit it off. But of course there may be no vacancy. Suppose I ring him up, not using your name of course."

After several tries he got Hastings on the telephone.

"If you could secure an extraordinarily fine English teacher, could you use him?" he asked.

After a moment he turned to Gavin. "His only vacancy is in history. Could you teach that?"

"If I had to," Gavin said slowly, "but English, of course, is my subject."

After further conversation on the phone Bob reported, "He's not too happy with his English department and thinks he might work out some sort of compromise with the history. He wants to see you, of course. He's in his office right now. Why not strike while the iron's hot?"

"You didn't give him my name?"

"No. I just told him he'd get a pleasant surprise."

"You always set things moving, Bob. How can I thank you?"

"Well, you haven't got the job yet, but there may be possibilities. And Gavin, let me know the news of the bride and groom. That whole thing hits me, somehow. I can imagine what it's done to you and Cecily. How's she holding up?"

"She's wonderful, always. Well, I'll go ahead and see this man and then let you know how the chips fall."

The High School building was impressively large and new, but as Gavin followed the sign that said *Principal's Office,* he made a wry face. "It *smells* like a public school," he thought. "Why is it that a college has a different odor?"

He found Hastings a large, comfortably corpulent man with ruddy cheeks and a friendly smile. Only his tired eyes gave away the secret that he had once dreamed of greater things. As he rose to greet Gavin, his face expressed amazement.

"Why Professor McAllister! I can't believe this. Our paths haven't really crossed, but of course I know you. Sit down and if you will I'd like you to tell me the story of why you're here. I'm sure there is one."

Gavin told it very briefly, dwelling chiefly on the matter of the degree.

"Yes," Hastings said, fiddling irritably with the paper knife, "that's what he would think of. He's a small man, Waring. It's a pity. In many ways he has held the College back from being a modern, first-class institution. Well, as to our unbelievable good fortune, I'll certainly juggle the classes around so that you will have practically all English, and I'll get the school board to stretch the salary as far as possible."

"There's one thing I must tell you, Mr. Hastings. I do need this job right now and if I get it I will do my very best, but I couldn't promise to keep it for more than this year. That is, I will be trying to get into my college work again. I want to be honest about this."

Hastings smiled. "I would guess that, if you hadn't told me, but I appreciate your frankness. To have you here even for a year would certainly give an impetus to our—dare I call it—academic life. And, as to me . . ."

He looked off out the window. "I've been in a bit of a slump lately. Just to have a chat with you often would give me a tremendous life. You see, English was my major also."

"How far did you go?"

"Master's."

Gavin reached his hand. "Shake," he said. "We're brothers under the skin, and I don't mind admitting to you that I haven't had too many chances for congenial talks on the English—classics, shall we say?"

"I understand, and thank you. Now, as far as I'm concerned you have the position here. I'll call a special meeting of the board at once. They are very amendable to my wishes so I don't think we'll have any trouble there unless it is with salary. Could you wait until I talk to them before I name it?''

Gavin rose. "You've been very kind and a load has been lifted. I admit I've had a heavy jolt, but a year here with you may compensate. Anyway, thanks again.''

He didn't stop to see Bob but called him on the phone.

"So far, so good, old man, and you're a wizard as usual. I like Hastings enormously. He's a man I can work with. A happy change from you know who! 'God moves in a mysterious way,' as you may have heard, so I'm going to take things as they come and try to be thankful.''

"Salary?'' Bob asked.

"That lies with the board. Hastings will let me know.''

"It's sure to be a good deal less than you were getting, but maybe not too far out of line. As you know, the Marsden trustees are pretty sticky.''

When Gavin told Cecily that night, she first blanched, then turned scarlet with anger. It somehow comforted Gavin to hear her, usually so gentle, burst into vituperation against Waring. All his own pent-up shock, disappointment and humiliation seemed now to have found a voice. He did not try to stop her until her tears began to flow and then he comforted her.

"This, on top of all you've given up," she kept repeating. "This is too much for you to bear, Gavin. My heart aches for you!"

"There," he said, "I feel better already. You've never even given a thought to how this may affect you."

"What do you mean?"

"Well, the salary will be a good deal smaller."

"Oh, that," she said. "We'll make out. That is the least of it."

He drew her close. "I can't tell you how much I love you. So let's just consider the matter closed."

Hastings called up after three anxious days had passed. He reported that the school board was unanimous in electing Gavin to the position. As to salary, the best they would offer would be seven thousand. Would he accept? He would. As a matter of fact, he felt too weary, too beaten down to start looking for anything else.

He began at once to work in his flower beds. The roses were having their first fine rapture of blooming, the lemon lilies were sweet, the madonnas ready to unfold. He cultivated, sprayed and weeded, saying to himself meanwhile: "All my hurts my garden spade can heal."

Then often with the quirk of a smile he would hold converse with the long gone author. "Not *all,* Mr. Emerson, you were wrong. Not *all,* but some. Yes, I'd even go so far as to say a good many!"

They watched for the postman with quick-beating hearts, and one day the letter came, addressed in Abe's handwriting. Gavin opened it nervously and Cecily sat close as they read:

DEAR MR. AND MRS. MCALLISTER:
  Here we are actually in Edinburgh at Miss Het's, who couldn't possibly be kinder to us. We had a smooth flight over but Rose was pretty tired when we got here. Miss Het put her right to bed and she slept the clock round twice, with Miss Het running in to look at her every hour or so to be sure she was all right. I explained about the busy ten days before we left, and that I thought sleep was just what she needed to relax her. Now she looks better and is ready to eat but willing to rest up a little

longer, so Miss Het fixes the trays and I take them up. She says she's coming downstairs tomorrow.

Miss Het can't look enough at Rose, and she keeps talking about you, Mr. McAllister, when you were a little boy, living with her. I'm happy to say she has sort of taken to me. I think she smells *old country* on me.

I've been over to the University and presented my records from Marsden and it seems I'll have no difficulty in getting registered and signed up for my classes.

This is a wonderful city. When Rose feels like it I want to take her to see some of the sights. I forgot to say I did as you suggested and found out at the University the name of a fine doctor. We'll get an appointment soon.

I know Rose will write a little later and meanwhile now, she sends her love. And may I too?

ABE

Six

GAVIN KEPT BUSY during the July weeks. There were the High School courses to go over with Hastings, a pleasant enough task, for the men enjoyed each other's company, and Gavin knew his suggestions were more than approved when the principal said one day that he felt as though an exhilarating mental breeze had sprung up. "I was getting sluggish," he added.

There were long talks with the Judge in which Gavin did most of the listening, for the old man was still unreconciled to Gavin's demotion. Sometimes he launched into eloquent denunciation of the trustees as men of no vision, no insight, no firmness of purpose. Again, scattering the rules of grammar to the winds and adding to the wreckage a few timely expletives, he would describe them hotly as lily-livered molly-coddles followin' Waring like a lot of

216

damned sheep, no spine, no guts and what in hell was the College comin' to if a thing like this could happen?

Gavin switched him off as soon as he could, the best means being a late letter from Rose which he read with few omissions. The change in the Judge was amazing. He relaxed in his big chair at once, eagerly intent upon the news.

"Just read that last part again, Gavin, about the sight seein'."

And Gavin would read: "We are getting to know some of the most famous spots of this beautiful city. We all go out together on the weekends. We walked up Princes Street last Saturday and saw the Scott monument, but the others wouldn't let me climb it. It's lovely just to look at, though. We've seen the flower clock. You will remember it, Daddy. And one evening we went to the castle and saw the soldiers marching in their kilts, playing the bagpipes. I knew then that I had a lot of Scottish blood in me. The music is weird but rouses something in me tremendously."

And once he read a letter from Abe himself: "I know Rose is writing you regularly but there may be some things I can tell you that she does not say. I was more anxious at first than I confessed, for I knew Rose was very unhappy. She was homesick and worried about everything. I did my best and Miss Het was still better. She is so bright and jolly and full of funny little stories and jokes. When Rose began to laugh I knew we were really making progress. She is taking an interest in the city now, and also in the house which is quaint, the kitchen being the coziest spot. I got a good comment on a paper last week and Rose seemed impressed for the first time. Of course that pleased me. I feel sure the doctor is a good one. He is an obstetrician, as you told me to get. Her visits to him I think cheer her up. She looks well now and seems to like going shopping with Miss Het. I couldn't enjoy my work more and I'm trying hard to justify your faith in me." In a postscript he added, "In every way."

"Does Rose ever mention Abe?" the Judge asked.

"Never."

"Give her time," the old man said sadly. "He's a good boy." Then he drew a long sigh. "We mustn't look the future too hard in the face. We must hold ourselves to the present. Poor child!" he always added. "Poor child."

Once he said, "Seen Loren Scott lately?"

"No, and I don't care to."

"Me neither, but I run into him the other day and there was no gettin' away. He looks poorly. He sent that young jackanapes of his over to Europe right after Commencement to travel an' *improve* himself! Of all fool things to do. He'd ought to have kept him at home and got him a job. He hain't got the stamina of a boiled oyster." Then he began to chuckle.

"I just read something yesterday about oysters—old Arab legend." He fell back again to his perfect English. "It seems they believe that one night in the month of April the oysters all rise to the surface of the water and bare their bosoms to heaven, as it were, until each has received a dewdrop. Then they return to their dark and misty deeps and out of the dewdrop each creates a pearl. Silly thing and yet somehow it caught my fancy. Much nicer idea than that a pearl is produced by irritation, as we've assumed. Also, if even in a legend oysters are endued with a sort of delicate intelligence there's hope for all of us, eh?"

Gavin always left the Judge, with his rich mind and varying grammar, with something interesting upon which to feed his own spirit, and just now he needed it. He had to admit also that the Judge's explosive wrath at Waring and the trustees, like that of Cecily's first reaction, was balm to his soul even though he tried to change the subject when the old man's face looked apoplectic. His talk with Devereux had been very different. The latter had heard the news by the faculty grapevine, but he listened in silence to Gavin's own explanation, his lips, set in a hard line, being the only sign of his feeling. At last he had said, "It's a dirty deal, Gavin, and makes me feel more than ever that I ought to leave Marsden. But I'm a coward. Or maybe just lazy." And he had left without further words.

Through the warm days, Gavin realized that he was learning for the first time what solitude could mean. Cecily, with some other mothers, was helping supervise a playground and swimming pool for little children so she and Cissie were away through the day, the boys each had jobs and picked up lunch where they were; Gavin was alone in his garden. Alone to think, while the mixed aromatic perfume from the flowers and the "live murmur of the summer day" surrounded him. It was indeed life itself and the meaning of it which he was questioning, but even his thinking seemed lacking in depth. Did the great majority of men, he wondered, live from day to day immersed in their work and the general trivia of living, without ever probing deeper to find out what really lay in their own hearts or in the mystery of the universe? And even if they did pause sometimes to consider the infinite possibilities of the cosmos, or of themselves, would the actualities of the present world not draw them quickly back again into its shallow grip?

As he looked into his own heart, in this new solitude, he found it was almost unbearably sad. The strength he had mustered during all the strain leading up to Rose's strange wedding was now dissipated. He had only a heavy weight of uneasiness. What if things went wrong? They could, even with a good doctor. And she was so far away. But the worst fear of all was that they might have condemned her (without the unpleasant business of divorce) to a loveless marriage. Perhaps in their other anxieties they had not given this sufficient thought. For Rose had never once named Abe in her letters. As she had pointed out to them, even if he loved her it did not follow that she could love him. As he, himself, knew, love could not be coerced. Suddenly even in his gloom his lips twitched in a smile. He was remembering a conversation he had overheard between the boys.

"Well, what's the matter with Jane Hand? She's a friend of Phoebe's and we could go out together on doubles. Why don't you date her?" Bruce had asked.

"Oh, I don't know."

"She's pretty enough."

"Oh, sure."

"And she's lots of fun."

"Sure."

"Well, what's wrong with her?"

"Nothing, but she just *doesn't turn me on!*"

That was it, Gavin thought. Like the song that echoed through the house in the virile young voices, day after day: "Come on, light my fire!" That was love. A spark, a flame, a fire. There must be this or there was nothing.

There was always, too, of course, the cruel disappointment of the loss of his degree when it seemed almost in wait for his grasp; there was the wounded pride of dropping from college to high school level. (I didn't know I had so much pride, he mused.) Even some favorite lines from Shelley which he had often quoted to Cecily through the years when things were hard seemed to have lost their potency for him.

*Many a green isle needs must be
In the deep wide sea of Misery . . .*

He felt now that the sea was very deep and the green isles few and far between. After a fortnight of his garden solitude, however, he began to feel his usual resiliency returning. His musing began to have a sort of felicity. He thought sometimes of the Judge's Arab legend of the oysters. The difference between a gritty irritant and a dewdrop in the little insides of a mollusk, causing the shining layers of a pearl, was great indeed.

"I've had irritation enough, God knows," he said aloud one day, with a laugh. "I might try a dewdrop."

At least he began to throw off his personal distress. He filled the house with fresh flowers for Cecily when she got home weary from her day with the youngsters; he went often to see Billy King and restock his larder. Billy brightened at sight of him, was eager to talk but usually bemused by drink. He was thinner too and complained of a shortness of breath. When Gavin urged calling a doctor Billy became violent. "Never!" he shouted.

"You know the first thing he'd tell me to do? Well, I won't do it, so that's that!"

Gavin often cooked him his dinner and stayed until he had finished it. He tried again taking Billy out for short drives, but oddly enough, as always, he didn't seem to enjoy them.

"Look at those harvest fields, Billy. Aren't they beautiful?"

"I'd rather see a French café for ten minutes than look at these for an hour. Thanks, though, just the same."

So Billy would return to his unkempt apartment with its shelf of books and Paris paintings on the walls.

One evening at dinner Gavin could tell that Cecily was agitated. When the house was quiet she told him the problem. Marie Devereux had called to her that afternoon as she was passing and begged her to come in. Cecily had sent little Cissie on with some other children and done so.

It seemed that Marie had fallen in with Devereux's plan of trying to bring Bunny and Schneider together. At the beginning it had seemed very romantic and in a way very funny. She and Dev had had many a laugh over their attempts to stir up a mutual interest. She had had the dinner party and had brightened up Bunny's appearance as Cecily might remember, but *now* . . .

"Well, what now?" Gavin questioned.

"The thing is," Cecily went on, "they've actually fallen in love, but Schneider doesn't want to marry apparently. She's sure he loves her. He goes to see her nearly every evening but seems to come no nearer the point. She thinks he just doesn't want to change his way of living. She's afraid he's never going to ask her, or else ask something against her principles, and meanwhile it's breaking her heart. So there's the situation."

"That's a funny thing about Schneider," Gavin said thoughtfully. "I would certainly never believe that he would entertain any but the most *honorable intentions* toward a woman. I think there's something in particular holding him back."

"Well, whatever it is, it's killing Bunny. Marie said she was the worst person to consult, for in Paris it would all be quite simple, especially at their age. But she added that in *Marsden, this prudish town,* as she termed it, nothing but marriage would do. And she wondered . . ."

"Wondered what?" asked Gavin hastily.

"She wondered if maybe *you* could talk to Schneider."

"Me?" Gavin exploded. "One man just doesn't go to another and say 'look, why don't you marry that woman?' I think Marie had a nerve to suggest this. Or did you?" he added, with a twinkle.

"No, I just said I'd tell you, but I approve of the idea so think it over. Bunny's going to break under this if something's not done soon. One thing I believe I will do. I'll give a little return party for the same group that Marie had, only make it all very simple because of the hot weather. Then you can have a chance to study your subjects at close range."

"When will you have it?"

"Oh, I believe next Sunday evening."

"That sounds nice, but don't expect me to counsel the lovelorn."

In spite of his disclaimers Gavin kept thinking about Schneider. He had great respect for the man—strong, self-contained, shy, immersed in his work, spending his leisure hours in a tiny laboratory he had built for himself at the back of his small house. Gavin could picture his not being eager to leave all this or to see a wife dusting his test tubes and vials (if she would!), but neither could he see Schneider going to see a woman nearly every evening giving an undeniable impression he was in love with her and yet not in any way declaring his feelings. There was something back of this.

On Saturday evening he asked Cecily suddenly, "Isn't this the night Bunny goes to her Forum Group?"

"Yes, it is. Why?"

"Oh, nothing. I'm glad she has one outside interest."

Then a little later he said he believed he'd return a book to the Judge. He didn't stay long there, however, but went on to where Schneider lived in his modest little brick house. On the doorstep he started twice to go back and then finally rang the bell. When Schneider came he fairly drew him inside.

"Why, McAllister! This is like a gift from heaven. I wanted to see . . . that is, I wanted to talk. Come in, come in."

Once seated, Gavin began on the usual amenities, but he could see Schneider was nervous, so he decided to make the break at once.

"You've heard of the kind of fools who rush in. Well, I'm like that, I'm afraid, but I've been thinking about you and wishing I could give you some advice."

"But I need advice. I'm a very unhappy man. Perhaps you can help me. Tell me what you came to say."

"It was just this. I have a most happy marriage, but we could so easily have lost some beautiful years by putting it off. As a matter of fact everything was against it at the time, but we went ahead anyway. Now, I could be quite wrong, but it looks a little to me as though you might be falling in love yourself . . ."

"But I am," interrupted Schneider. "I'm in love for the first time in my life, but I can't get any further."

"Why not?" Gavin asked.

"Well, you see I've never had anything to do with women outside of an unfortunate experience when I was young, and I'm afraid of them. I mean of marriage. I've lived a sort of celibate life. I'm afraid of myself. I don't know whether I'd be . . . adequate. I'm just plain scared, McAllister."

Gavin laughed, which somehow seemed to cheer his host.

"You don't think it could be too serious then?" Schneider demanded.

"Nonsense!" said Gavin heartily. "Listen. When you were a kid, did you go swimming?"

"Of course."

"So did I. I can picture us yet. Skinny

little snipes standing above the deep hole, shivering and shaking, all of us scared to death. Then at last we'd jump in and come up snuffling and laughing and yelling and as proud as Punch. Schneider, all you need is to take the plunge and you'll be the happiest man in the world."

"You think there would be no danger of my . . ."

"Your only danger is to delay until you've worn both yourself and Dr. Foster out with 'hope deferred.' I repeat it, take the plunge at once, man!"

"She's out tonight," Schneider said, a new note of determination in his voice.

"You're coming to supper at our house tomorrow evening, you know. You'll see her then. And I do hope you will forgive my effrontery in offering advice. It was really . . ."

"But I can't ever thank you enough. I was in despair and I couldn't have *gone* to anyone, don't you see? If you hadn't opened up the subject I'd never have unburdened myself. Now you must be best man at our wedding."

"I'll do that with pleasure, and now I must be getting home."

When he had left, however, he returned to

stick his head in the door. "Make the most of your opportunities, now, Schneider," he said.

The supper party was a success except for the fact that Bunny was pale, and quiet. Schneider, on the contrary, seemed bursting with health, spirits and loquacity. No one had ever known him to be so jovial and interesting before. Except for Bunny everyone was in a gay and talkative mood. Between the sallies and the laughter there were many questions about the bride and groom and how they were enjoying Edinburgh. The surprise and interest of the town in general was repeated and commented upon.

"Well," said Marie, "I knew when Abe sang the 'Serenade' in the play that there was a real love affair afoot. Those lines

'Oh, hear my longing cry!
Oh, love me or I die'

were certainly not just . . .''

And at that point Bunny, very quietly and gracefully as though it had been rehearsed, slipped from her chair to the floor.

Schneider was beside her in a second. "Get a doctor! Get a doctor! She's dead!" he cried frantically.

"It's just a faint, Dr. Schneider. Carry her in to the couch. She'll soon be all right. It's the heat. I'll get some spirits of ammonia," Cecily said.

"I'll bring some brandy," Gavin said quickly.

"Don't worry, Schneider," Devereux kept saying. "Did you never see a woman faint before?"

"Never!" said Schneider, his own face pale. "I wish you'd get a doctor in a hurry. She looks like death itself. We've got to find out . . ."

He knelt down beside the couch and laid his ear to Bunny's heart, listening. As he did so Bunny stirred, opened her eyes, he raised his head and she, seeing it close beside her own, put her arms around his neck and kissed him. "Oh, Herman!" she said.

Schneider blushed scarlet but after a second returned the kiss, then rose and looking at the silent, watchful group made the quite unnecessary statement, "I think she has regained consciousness."

She had. She sniffed the ammonia and drank the brandy while a most charming rosy color slowly crept into her cheeks. She sat up at last full of apologies for disturbing the supper.

"But we were all finished except for dessert," Cecily assured her. "We are just so relieved you feel better again, and we can have . . ."

"I think, Mrs. McAllister, I should take Dr. Foster home at once, if you will excuse us," Schneider said firmly.

Marie's delicately accented voice rose distinctly. "You are quite right, Dr. Schneider. There is just one thing which should be considered. I don't believe Hilda should be left alone tonight. She *might* have another recurrence of the faint, or for some reason need a doctor. We are all rather involved with our families, but you are free. Couldn't you stay with her? She has a very comfortable couch in her study."

There was an almost perceptible holding of breaths and then Schneider said, looking not at Marie but at Gavin, "Yes, I think I'll do that."

With which announcement he picked up Bunny, a mere feather weight, in his arms, and after she had made her good-byes, carried her to his car and drove off.

When they were gone the others settled to a delicious discussion of the evening's events.

"And did you see how she looked when her face colored up? I wouldn't have believed it but she was actually *pretty!*" Colby said, adding, "her nose never twitched once."

"I've always said," Devereux put in, "that all Bunny needed to change her from a dried-up professor of dead languages to a full blooming woman, was a *lover!* And by Gad, I think she's got one."

"She's got something much better," Gavin said. "I think she's got herself a husband."

"And the way you suggested his staying there tonight, Marie," Cecily laughed, "as though it was the most conventional thing in the world."

"And so it may be," Marie answered, "but one can hope."

The talk grew hilarious, but even while they "made book" on the date of the wedding there was an undercurrent of satisfaction and esteem for the two principals. It was very late when the dessert was finally remembered and eaten and then the guests all marched out to Lohengrin, which Cecily began to play.

When they were gone, she sat on at the piano with her head bowed. "I did it without thinking," she said chokingly, "and now all that Rose missed, that *we* missed too, though that's not so important, suddenly sweeps over me. Oh, Gavin, does it still hurt you so?"

"Yes," he replied quietly. "But the very fact of your playing that spontaneously was a good sign. It shows we can both rise above it. And there is always hope."

Before she slept Cecily said, "You know, Gavin, I can read you like a book."

"I know. It's disconcerting to have a wife who guesses your very thoughts."

"Do you think you would like me to be different?"

"You know what I think of you and I'll be glad to give you immediate and convincing proof if you wish."

Cecily giggled. "No, thanks. It's pretty late. What I meant was I knew last night you were going to see Schneider. That business of returning a book to the Judge wasn't convincing."

"But I did that."

"Then went on to Schneider's?"

"Yes."

"Whatever did you say to him? He was certainly a changed man tonight."

"Oh, when I found he was really in love I counseled against delay in marriage."

"You must have done a good job. I'm so happy for Bunny."

"And I'm glad for Schneider. I think he's been a very lonely man."

The little group had been right in their predictions that the wedding would come soon. Devereux, hitting the date exactly, collected his bets and told them all not to gamble with a professional. The ceremony was simple and dignified in Bunny's own apartment with Gavin as best man, Marie as matron of honor, and a few special faculty friends as guests. Marie had let herself go on Bunny with the effect of creating a charmingly soignée and beautifully gowned woman.

While there had been an honest effort to respect the couple's wish for secrecy, the news had leaked out. So, as soon as the caterer had finished serving the supper, there were shouts outside, a great strumming of guitars and the voices of a dozen or so town students raised in what purported to be song: "Come on, light my fire!" The cheerful rock and roll blasted the quiet of the evening and added the final authentic touch to the occasion with: "Somewhere my love!"

There were calls finally for the bride and groom and Schneider and Bunny stepped out on the porch of the apartment amid boisterous acclaim. To the surprise of the guests, Schneider was apparently expecting the serenade and ready for it. He called the leader and pressed some bills into his hand.

"Now all of you go down to The Pantry and have a good treat from my wife and me!"

There were thanks and hurrahs and the gradually receding sounds of voices and guitars. "Somewhere my love . . ."

The Schneiders, it was learned, were leaving the next day for an extended European tour, so the farewells and good wishes were spoken that night.

"You know, Devereux," Gavin said as they all walked down the street, "for anyone with as low a motive as you had at the beginning, you've come out with an amazingly fine ending. I really congratulate you."

"Ah," said Devereux in his most elegant voice, "as the great bard of Avon would say, 'The course of true love doth *sometimes* run quite smooth.'"

But in the McAllister home during the days which followed it seemed that the original Shakespearean statement was the more truthful one. For it was apparent that something was badly wrong with Bruce. Always the best-natured and most cheerful of all the children, fount of all jokes and witticisms, he was all at once irritable, dark-browed and for the most part silent. After several days of this Gavin cornered him in the hall.

"Bruce, I know something's wrong. Can't you confide in me? Have you and Phoebe quarreled?"

"Good God no!" he answered almost with violence. "The thing is . . . I might as well tell you. I guess I've just been thinking if I don't talk about it, it won't happen, but it's going to. Mr. Henderson has been transferred to the California office and the family has to leave in about ten days. He's rushing them off. And Dad, *I can't bear it!*"

Gavin's face was full of pain. "Oh, my dear boy," he said.

"You're not going to tell me then that I'm too young to know what love is?" Bruce said harshly.

"No, I'm not."

"Nor that if Phoebe goes to California I'll find another girl I'll love just as much?"

Gavin shook his head. "No, I couldn't honestly say that. First love cuts very deep."

The boy seemed to relax a little. "If you'd given me those old clichés I might have done something I'd have regretted. I can talk to you, now. Have you any ideas at all?"

"Well," Gavin said thoughtfully, "we might stretch finances and let you go out to California as near Phoebe as possible and take your Senior year. In that way you could go on seeing each other."

"But that's just it. We couldn't. Her father will hardly let her see me here. He hates me. I think he'd hate anybody that was in love with her. So if I went out there it would make him furious. And of course we're both under age," he added.

"Bruce, my heart aches for you. If there is ever anything I can do, tell me. Meantime be as brave as you can."

The boy rested his head for a second against his father's shoulder. "I'm glad you're the way you are, Dad," he said, and went out.

When Gavin explained the situation to Cecily she was full of distress. "And Phoebe is such a darling little thing. Of course after a time Bruce is sure to find another girl . . ."

"Don't!" Gavin said. "The man who wrote 'Deep as first love' knew what he was talking about. If I had been losing you and anyone had tried to comfort me with what you just said, I'd have knocked him down."

"Why, Gavin, would you really?"

"I would, and furthermore I think if I had

said that to Bruce just now in his present state of mind he would have taken a lunge at me. But it's a sad business.''

"It's a sad business having children," Cecily said with a sigh. "Beautiful, but sad. By the way, did you notice that in Rose's last letter she mentioned Abe once. It didn't mean much, for you know she just said, 'Aunt Het and Abe have been painting the kitchen.' But still it's the first time she's named him at all.''

There seemed so little they could do for Bruce as the days passed and they watched the anguish on his young face. Cecily cooked all his favorite foods, which were most of the time uneaten; Gavin by a word or a gesture, whenever he could, showed the depth of his sympathy. But they knew under the circumstances there was no hope. When the time of the Hendersons' departure was very near, Bruce asked his father for the car on Friday.

"I've got a day off from my job, and Mother, if you'll pack us a lunch we'll go off on a long day's jaunt.''

"Good idea," Gavin said, feeling the inadequacy of the comment.

Bruce looked tense as he drove off that morning. "Don't worry if I'm late," he said. "We're going to make a full day of it.''

They did, for at two in the morning he was not back. Cecily was anxious and wakened her husband. "They might have had an accident," she breathed.

"Oh, Bruce is a good driver. They're just making the day last as long as possible. Go back to sleep."

They did not hear the car drive in, nor footsteps on the stairs. Breakfast was the usually late and luxurious one ordained for Saturday. Ian came down about ten, ate his and set off to work on a friend's car. Eleven came and noon was approaching when Cecily exclaimed over Bruce's delay. "I don't know when to put the muffins in the oven. I made them because he's so fond of them."

Gavin jumped up from his book. "I didn't realize it was so late. I'll go up and rout him out at once. He's had enough sleep by this time."

He went up to Bruce's room and tapped on the door. "Hi there, lazy bones! It's nearly twelve o'clock." He pushed the door open and then stopped dead on the threshold. There were two heads on the pillows.

Bruce sat up and drew Phoebe beside him. "Dad, this is my wife. We drove down to

West Virginia yesterday and got married. We *had* to," he said, and then laughed. "I don't mean it that way. We just couldn't stand it to be separated and I wanted to come right back here and tell you and Mother. I do hope you'll . . . I mean . . . I hope . . ."

Two pairs of eyes looked at Gavin, beseechingly. He walked over to the bed, kissed Phoebe and grasped his son's hand. "This is certainly a big surprise, I admit, but I think it's going to prove a nice one. Now, I'll go down and prepare your mother. She's been waiting to put the muffins in the oven, so if you two will get dressed quickly and come down we'll hear all the news while you have breakfast."

He started for the door, but Bruce jumped out of bed and overtook him. Oddly enough he looked taller and broader in his pajamas than in his daytime clothes. His eyes were swimming as he caught his father's arm.

"Dad, I can't tell you . . . I can't thank you enough. I was worried of course as to how . . . Oh Dad, I do thank you!"

Gavin patted his back as though he were a little boy. "Listen," he said, "you go back and tell that pretty little wife of yours how glad we are to have her in the family."

He couldn't see too clearly himself as he

went out and closed the door behind him. He stood for a few moments on the upper landing, his hand grasping the banister as though he were in danger of falling. Then he wiped his eyes and went down to Cecily. He made her sit down but smiled into her startled face as he briefly gave her the facts. She turned pale but made no outcry, just kept looking at him as though for strength.

"This is the way you are taking it, Gavin?"

"This is the way I'm taking it. There is no other. On the whole I think the thing is good."

It was really a gay breakfast, for Bruce now was not only restored in spirits but elated beyond all bounds; Phoebe's soft brown eyes were shining with joy and incredulity over her welcome and Gavin and Cecily played up as best they could. When Ian came loping casually in he took one look at the young couple and shouted, "What's all this about?"

"My wife!" Bruce stated proudly, "and you'd better treat me with respect from now on, young fellah."

There was but one dark cloud. Bruce had called the Hendersons the night before to say they were belated and Phoebe would stay at his home overnight. Now, he must go and tell her parents the truth. "And I'm scared," he confided to his father. "I honestly don't know what that man may do to me. He's really savage."

"Would you like me to go with you?"

"Yes, you bet I would, but I don't think it would look well. This is my own business and I'll have to face up to it. Just wish me luck."

When he came back his face looked drawn but there was the light of the victor in his eyes. "It was a pretty rough hour," he told his father, "but I think the man has actually come around a little. For one thing I've never once had a chance before to talk to him and he seemed impressed that I could speak the English language fluently. Phoebe and I are to go down to see the family tomorrow afternoon to say good-bye. So I hope the worst is over. Whew! I wouldn't like to go through that again!"

When Cecily was relaxing from the excitement, the young folks in their room discussing Bruce's recent encounter with Mr. Henderson, and Ian joyfully off to spread the word amongst his contemporaries, Gavin went to see the Judge. He found him in a dark mood.

"An aged man is but a paltry thing,
A tattered coat upon a stick . . ."

he began, as greeting.

"Unless soul clap its hands and sing,"

Gavin went on, smiling. "You should always finish a quotation. Well, I've brought you some news that will make you feel young. You know Bruce has been desperately in love for a couple of years with little Phoebe Henderson. Her father is a Victorian or worse. Never treated Bruce civilly. His office has been changed to California and the family leaves in a few days. Poor Bruce has been beside himself."

The Judge was leaning forward now, his eyes piercing Gavin's. "Well?" he said sharply.

"This morning when I went up to Bruce's room to wake him I found Phoebe beside him. They had driven down to West Virginia yesterday and been married."

"Oh, no!" the Judge groaned. "No! What did you *do?*"

"What do you suppose I'd do? I kissed the bride and shook hands with the groom."

"In bed?" The Judge's tone was one of pure shock.

"Well," Gavin grinned, "that's where they happened to be at the moment."

"This is monstrous," the Judge bellowed. "You've got to get this annulled, Gavin. You can't take this on after all you've been through. I won't let you. You've had enough, God knows, without assuming the responsibility of a lovesick young calf and a silly girl. Why there may even be . . . be issue!"

"I believe it happens sometimes," Gavin replied. "In this case they are both Seniors and I think they'll finish college and Bruce will get settled in a job before they start a family. However . . ."

"You'd better put in the *however*."

"Well, Cecily and I are not old. We like babies!"

"Gavin, you're the biggest fool I've ever met."

"Maybe. But now calm down and listen to my side, Judge. Of course I would not have chosen for Bruce to marry now, and certainly at first it was a shock. But this is the way I look at it. My son has married the girl he loves with honor and brought her back to *his own room* for their wedding night. He could have gone to some cheap motel, but he wanted to bring her home. In a sense he wanted to bring her back *to us*. I'm glad to say we didn't fail him. As I think it all over it seems rather sweet to me.''

''Nonsense! You're crazy!''

''Phoebe is a lovely young girl. She's a fine cook, too, Bruce says, having had to do most of the dinners since her mother got home late from interminable bridge games. This will be the greatest comfort to Cecily who looks a bit tired and could use a little help this summer. Also there will be a young girl's voice again in the house . . .''

He couldn't go on.

''Well, well,'' the Judge said at last, blowing his nose, ''tell those two young idiots when they get over billin' and cooin' a little to come down to see me. I'll have a little present for them. I s'pose they could use it. Get along, then, Gavin, and let me be thinkin' this thing over. I s'pose you believe all that tommyrot about *first love,* then?''

Gavin nodded. ''Hastings at the High School has a fine taste in poetry. We've been reading together sometimes this summer. The other day we came upon a sonnet. Give me a bit of paper and I'll write you two lines that are apropos to the situation.''

"You can save yourself the trouble. I can't understand a livin' haet about your romantic stuff."

"Oh, this is plain enough. You can mull over it after I've gone." He wrote:

And blest the first sweet pain, the first
  most dear
Which burned my heart when Love came
  in as guest.

When he had reached the door the Judge called to him.

"I still think you're a damned fool, but just now we could mebbe perhaps use a few more fools like you."

Gavin only laughed and went on.

The advent of Phoebe into the McAllister household brought unexpected happiness. It was not only noticeable in the beaming and tender eyes of the bride and groom themselves, but it was as though this young joy leavened with light the unavoidable sorrow still in the hearts of Gavin and Cecily. Even Rose's letters after she heard the news had more warmth as she and Bruce had always been very close and she liked Phoebe.

As to Phoebe herself, when she had lost

her first shyness she revealed a charming and delicate humor, which coupled with Bruce's more lusty one kept waves of laughter running through the house. Much of the recent sadness and regrets seemed to be driven out as by magic, and on the more practical side Phoebe's eager desire to be helpful gave Cecily the rest she needed. As Gavin had predicted, a small, sweet voice rang out now upstairs and down and brought no hurt since it was so different from that of their own daughter.

One of Rose's letters was very wistful. "I did feel pretty sad when I read about the party and how beautifully it came off. I'm afraid I wept a little weep to think I wasn't there. But Abe took me out to a nice place to dinner and then to a funny play, so that helped."

The implication of the last statement, the first of its kind, meant much more to Gavin and Cecily than the party itself to which she referred. It had, indeed, turned out to be an astonishing success with thirty young people lounging about the rooms with half as many guitars, making the hours delightfully hideous with sounds of their own choosing, and eating every scrap of the food Cecily and Phoebe had prepared. There were gifts, too, and all sorts of clever speeches and advice to the newlyweds. So it had been set down by all as "a good party," though hardly, as Gavin and Cecily confessed to each other afterwards, their idea of a wedding reception even for the young.

"But it was fun," Cecily maintained stoutly. "And as long as Bruce and Phoebe are happy over it . . ."

One evening Bob St. Clair called up to ask if the lovebirds were at home. They were going out later but would certainly wait to see him. When he arrived he had a large package tied with white ribbons which he laid on Phoebe's knee. She opened it nervously to find rows of shining flat silver. Quick tears come at the unexpected beauty before her, and she had to allow Bruce to voice the first thanks. Then together they exclaimed and admired, their young faces flushed with pleasure.

"I'll have it engraved for you," Bob said, "as soon as you decide whether you want a monogram or just an initial. Think it over and tell me. Maybe you really should wait until you see if you get some more, then this can be exchanged for something else."

"Oh, I couldn't *ever* give this up," Phoebe said almost in fright and Bob insisted this was the most perfect piece of thanks he had ever heard. When they had placed a setting on the table to admire from every angle, they finally put the pieces back in their velvet case and bright with their happiness said their good-byes.

"And I'm *Uncle Bob,* remember," he told Phoebe. "I just needed an extra niece worse than anything, and congratulations, Bruce, on the one you gave me."

When they had left Gavin and Cecily expressed their own thanks and chatted on about the children, the party and Rose's letter. Cecily was knitting a tiny sweater and, seeing Bob's eyes upon it, she said, "Don't mention this until we tell you, will you?"

"Certainly not," he answered.

"Oh, you know that book on the Civil War I recommended, Bob? It's one of the best. I'll run up to the study and get it for you."

But Gavin found it had been misplaced, and it took longer than he had expected to find it. When he had it at last he went down, his slippered feet on the thickly carpeted stairs making no sound.

By the newel post he could see into the living room. Within it there was silence. The light was shining on Cecily's tawny hair and lovely face. Her lips were half parted in a smile. Her eyes, still long lashed, were bent over the tiny garment. And on Bob's face was a dark, intense, unmistakable look of love as he watched her. It went through Gavin like a sword.

He turned and softly retraced his steps, waiting above until his own heart was quieter and something perhaps had changed below. When he came down again he dropped the book with a crash, picked it up with an exclamation and then entered the room.

"Well," said Bob, "if the tome is as heavy as that, I don't know whether I want to read it. But give it to me. When my mind is too full of the toils of the law, it may prove an antidote. Say, I ought to be getting on. I always stay too long. And I must say that in spite of the way Bruce went about it, he's brought you a little prize."

He got up and said his good-nights as usual, slapping Gavin on the back, giving Cecily a light kiss on the cheek. "That's for the mother-in-law of the bride," he said, and in a few moments they heard his steps on the walk, the sound of the car, and he was gone.

Gavin and Cecily both sat down, she resuming her knitting and Gavin watching her. At last he said, "Darling, I made a discovery tonight that has upset me. I don't know whether I should tell you or not but I think I will. I came downstairs once before I let the book fall and that time I could see Bob's face as he looked at you. I think he . . . I think he is in love with you."

"I know," she said quietly. "I've known for some time."

"And you've never told me?"

"How could I," she said, "when he is your best friend?"

Then suddenly she leaned forward and put her face in her hands. She was weeping. "Oh, Gavin, what do you want me to do?" It sounded to him like a cry of anguish.

He sat for some minutes, stunned, while her tears continued; then he rose, went upstairs, collected his night things and went into Rose's room. He flung himself fully dressed upon the bed while over and over her words beat upon his brain. *What do you want me to do?* There was to be then, a choice, and he, Gavin, was to make it. No, his very soul shouted his rebellion. It was all madness, a nightmare that would disappear with the morning light. No such thought could ever come between him and Cecily. Why was he here, alone, running off like a frightened schoolboy? Why had he not spoken out strongly, casually, in answer to her strange question? He would get up and go back to her. He would dry her tears and tell her . . .

But he did not get up. He lay very still, indeed, as though all strength had left him. For there was a choice, unavoidably, inevitably. There was he, Gavin, himself, a school teacher, not even now a college professor. All the ardent young dreams of heading the English department in a great university as *Doctor McAllister* had faded and died with the years. He was teaching in a public school on a small salary.

And Bob? Handsome, debonair, socially-elect not only in Marsden but in the city as well, wealthy by inheritance and from the outstanding success of his own profession, a man both of charm and integrity, and he loved Cecily. All this he would lay at her feet if she were free, and how could *any* woman resist him? Marsden was a very old town, rooted in uprightness of tradition, but the modern world had edged in. Many of the most prominent citizens had exchanged one set of marriage vows for another. And the shock that he, himself, always felt over this was not, he knew, shared by the majority. He had until these moments felt so far removed from danger, so impervious to emotional disaster, that he had but looked objectively upon the disruption of other families in the town.

And Cecily? She had kept from him the knowledge of Bob's feeling and gone on giving freely, bravely, of her love to him, her husband. It was only now at this sudden crossroads of the heart that she had allowed herself that cry, that question . . . surely that confession.

He rose at last and walked over to the easy chair by the window. The chair had been Rose's big Christmas gift two years ago. He drew his breath sharply. They had all been so happy then before these various waves of darkness had settled upon their spirits. He sat down, viewing the present situation from every angle, wrestling on and on with the Angel until, torn and spent with the struggle, he knew that he loved his wife better than himself. He loved her enough to give her up if that was to be her happiness. Even as he knew his capability for this sacrifice the thought crossed his mind that if he were strong and powerful in his own professional success he might say instead, "Never! I will hold you against the world." But he couldn't say this, not as he was now, humiliated and bitterly disappointed with the future all uncertain before him. Not now.

He heard a soft sound in the doorway, and a slow white wraith entered. At once, automatically, he rose as though it were a stranger. As, indeed, at the moment it seemed to him to be. He made no move to go nearer but waited as Cecily crossed the room to him. From her voice he could tell she had been sobbing.

"Gavin," she began, "what is the matter? Why did you leave me and come in here?"

"I had to be alone. I had to think."

"About what? Oh, Gavin, you *couldn't* believe I had in any way encouraged Bob. You surely don't believe such a thing as that."

"No, I don't, but your question of course startled me."

"My question?" She sounded bewildered. "You mean about what you would want me to do? But you really are the one to decide. Shall I go on as I've been doing, never letting him guess that I know? Or . . . I know men feel differently about these things . . . do you want me to be rather cold and reserved with him and sort of make it plain we don't want him to keep on coming? But I'm so *sorry* for him. He's often said this is the only taste of

255

family life he has. It all seems so sad to me."

"Darling," Gavin began, "I know now that your innocent and loyal heart has never realized that there is a choice implicit in all this situation. That's what I've been thinking of here, all alone. I can tell you now honestly that I want your happiness above my own. I want you to think seriously now of all Bob has to offer you . . . to give you, forgetting me completely."

"To offer me!" she repeated. "To *give* me! Gavin, I think you're ill. In your sober senses you surely know that all the gold of the Indies could never tempt me away from you because I . . ."

But the sentence was never finished, for his lips were close upon hers.

Seven

THE NEXT MORNING alone at breakfast they talked over all the strange events of the night before and their full significance. After their mutual confessions their love had not then been expressed vocally.

"You know, Gavin," Cecily said now, "I'm not so sure that I like this great sacrificial part about your being willing to give me up. I think, even if you doubted me—and I'll never forgive you for that—you should have said, 'You behave yourself or I'll wring your little neck,' and told the man, *any* man in such a case, to go fly a kite or words to that effect."

Gavin was sober. "But you're forgetting one thing, darling. If any husband believed his wife was in love with another man, would he try to force her to stay with him? Yet here comes in the matter of principle. I don't believe any spouse should ever leave a mate

257

just because a glamorous newcomer has come upon the scene. That's what I firmly *believe,* yet when it came to you, all I could think of was your happiness. You do understand this, don't you?''

"I guess so. But I still believe I prefer the rough approach.''

Gavin laughed. "Very good. From now on I'll be rough and tough and beat you every few weeks to show what a strong guy I am, brooking no nonsense.''

But in spite of their teasing words, a new aura of love seemed to have fallen upon them. Not even as a bridegroom had Gavin been so tender, so untiring in his devotion. A delicacy, a sweet hesitancy like that of undeclared lovers, lay upon them. They forgot that as their eyes clung or as Cecily's arm stole around her husband's neck that these fresh evidences of their emotions would be noticed until Ian made a blunt remark one day.

"And would you please tell me just which is the bride and groom in the family? I declare it's hard to decide.''

"There are two,'' his father said promptly. "Your mother and I still qualify in many respects. And sometime—I hope not for quite a few years—you'll join the group, Ian.''

"And don't forget Rose!"

Cecily spoke quickly. "We never forget Rose. Sometimes I feel she is more in my thoughts than you all are who are right here. She's well and Abe is doing wonderfully in his courses. And I think you boys ought to write often to her. Letters mean so much."

"I wrote yesterday," Phoebe said gently, "just to fill in until Bruce gets time."

"That was nice of you," Gavin said, "but don't let that husband of yours off too easily."

And the weeks moved on toward September when there fell in the late afternoons what Gavin always called *the golden light*. It was not at all like the ambient sunshine which flooded the garden through the summer days. This was a strong, slanting splendor from the western sun which struck through the trees and fell in a kind of glory on the lawn and flowers. He was watching this one afternoon as he called to Cecily from the garden.

"How about tea out here? We can pretend we're in England."

She leaned, smiling, over the porch rail. "Wonderful. I'll make cucumber sandwiches to complete the illusion."

They ate at the small rustic table that stood next to the bed of phlox, with its delicate summer perfume.

"Are you finding it difficult to drive on the left side here in England?" Cecily remarked conversationally.

"Oh no," Gavin replied in kind. "I drove a lorry round here some, during the last war."

"The war!" Cecily's face paled. "Oh, what is going to happen to our boys now? I know we agreed to keep it out of our conversation with them so they wouldn't have to live it over twice, as it were, but they are not fools. They probably keep quiet about it to protect us. What do you think will come next, Gavin? It has all drawn so close."

"The only reason we've discussed it so little ourselves is that we've had so much else to worry about. Of course the thing that saved Abe was his going on to do graduate work. His marks were so high the board gave him a second exemption. And even after this he still may not be called. Good teachers with Master's degrees are not too plentiful. Of course we can't count on that. Ian, poor Ian, *lucky* Ian, is safe from active fighting. He has the slight limp, and though he tries never to admit it, that gammy leg tires before the other. It's Bruce I'm thinking most about, of course. He's put in for the university fellowship for advanced study, and with his grades he may possibly get it. If he does, he'll be close to home and the draft board will maybe take an interest in the plan and let him go through with it. But that's unpredictable. All we can do is wait and pray. But it's a bad, sad mess, and I can't even yet get a majority opinion in my own mind about the whole thing. In the last war at least we knew exactly what we were fighting for."

"I saw Mrs. Wilson today. Lester Scott's mother was her niece and she has tried to keep track of him. She says he has to be back home in order to get to camp by September fifteenth. Mr. Scott has tried every possible way to get him off, even to attempting to bribe a couple of the draft board, I guess, which made them furious. Mrs. Wilson says the news leaked out that Lester never finished his work and so never got his diploma and the draft board is adamant and she hopes they'll remain so. She thinks the Army will straighten Lester out if anything can. But she says Mr. Scott is beside himself. This is the first thing that his money can't buy."

"About time," Gavin said bitterly.

"And I had a feeling as I talked with her that maybe she suspected the truth about Rose's marriage and about . . . about Lester. She rather made a point of telling me that she had watched his actions very carefully, finding out what she could. She held my hand closely and I almost told her everything, but I didn't."

"I'm certainly glad you didn't. We've been fortunate that the town accepted it all with the casualness they did. I think we owe Bob quite a debt for that. He talked a lot about it, the *romance* part, after the play, and made the pieces all fit together. He did what we couldn't have done."

"I believe," Cecily said consideringly, "that the best thing for us all just now in connection with Bob is to ask him to dinner. I would like to have the Hastings before school opens. She's a very attractive little thing and I'd enjoy knowing them both better. We could ask another couple and if I can scare up an odd woman we could have some bridge. What do you think?"

"Very good. I think, as always, you are percipient. Fine word. To see Bob in a group right now will be easier than talking to him by himself. A little later we will have forgotten all about the problem. I hope.''

''And there's this, Gavin. Having the Hastings here *first* before they have us, is putting you in your proper place in relation to him.''

''Don't say *above* him for heaven's sake!''

''Well, I won't say it, but you see what I mean.''

''You're a naughty little schemer and on strength of that I'll have another cup of tea.''

Bringing up between them now the subject of the war was only allowing the dark cloud to become visible. As the family problems had beaten upon their hearts, and also because there was a temporary hiatus as it were for both Bruce and Abe, Gavin had found himself in what he felt was a cowardly condition: filling the days with the duties at hand, even the thoughts relating to the present, while he pushed back as much as possible the blackness of the distant scene. One reason for his reluctance to look it in the face was, as he had said to Cecily, because he was not sure what he believed. He had known war himself as a very young man. He had gone then, strongly, purposefully, sacrificially if it had to be, but for a

263

cause he felt to be definite and just. He would do so again or even send his son, which was inconceivably harder. But this indecisiveness of purpose was to him almost unendurable. As he talked to other men he found most of them evasive about their opinions.

"I'm absolutely against it," a man would say, "and yet when you take into consideration . . ." and so on and on.

He went one afternoon to see the Judge. After giving him the general family news he broached his problem.

"I've come to the place, Judge, where I've got to decide what I think about this war. It seems to me quite likely that Bruce will have to go next summer and possibly Abe too. I can't straddle a fence in my own mind any longer. Is this war right and necessary, with the end justifying the means? Or is it an egregious mistake leading nowhere but further disaster? You've always sidestepped a definitive answer yourself when I've tried to bring the matter up. Now, won't you tell me what you really think?"

The Judge settled back in his chair, with eyes half closed, and proceeded to answer obliquely as he often did.

"Never miss a chance to read anything

written by Chief Justice Holmes, Gavin. If I had an idol it would be that man. Vivid personality, keen sense of humor, great jurist and great philosopher. I keep a book of quotes from his writings here on my desk all the time. Here's one for you when you run into religious discussion. He says, 'I don't see why a man should despair because he doesn't see a beard on his Cosmos.' Isn't that beautiful? Isn't that perfect?" the Judge chuckled.

Gavin was serious. "You're turning my question aside as you always do."

"Now just hold your horses. I don't know a damned bit more about this war than you do. Nobody does. The hawks and the doves both squawk but they don't know either. The thing is here and at the time we're stuck with it, but I've got an answer for you. Or rather it's Justice Holmes' answer. Listen to this." He drew a book toward him, turned the pages and read:

"I do not know what is true. I do not know the meaning of the universe. But in the midst of doubt, in the collapse of creeds, there is one thing I do not doubt, and that no man who lives in the same world with most of us can doubt, and that is that the faith is true and adorable which leads a soldier to throw away his life in obedience to a blindly accepted duty, in a cause which he little understands, in a plan of campaign of which he has no notion, under tactics of which he does not see the use.

"That's the only answer I can give you, Gavin. I read every bit I can find about Vietnam. I look at every picture and listen to every report. The sheer courage of the men out there is beyond belief. For the time being, when I can do nothing else, I'm going to concentrate on that. And you'd better too. There's something so big going on out there that it dwarfs the right or wrong of the war itself. That's how I feel." He put the book back in its place.

Gavin sat silent for a few minutes and then stood up and grasped the old man's hand. "Thanks, Judge. You've given me something to hold on to, even though perhaps I don't go the whole way with you. I'll stop torturing myself about my indecision though."

"Does Rose ever mention Abe?" the Judge asked abruptly.

"Yes, once in a while very casually.

"Always in connection with Aunt Het."

"Well, that's something. The little lovebirds here doing well?"

"Wonderfully. Phoebe is a delight to have around."

"Nice child. You may have been right, Gavin. As the Scots say about young marriages, 'better to make a spoon than spoil a horn.' And how many of your friends would know what *that* means?"

"Mighty few. And if I recall I taught that proverb to you myself."

"Oh, get along with you," the Judge answered amiably.

As he drove slowly back Gavin noted the red of the dogwood trees and the bronze of the grape leaves which hung over a trellis here and there. It was nearly time for school. He still hated the thought, though there was one consoling feature. He and his family were still in Marsden. He had grown fond of the place as he knew Cecily had done. It was home. They had loved and laughed, had suffered and, in some ways at least, triumphed here. Here they had watched the children through their young years. No other place would ever be the same to them as this in which they had experienced the strange, sweet, poignant years of their family's adolescence. Of course little Cissie was yet to approach them. If only a position could open up for him here that would be worthy of what he honestly felt he had to offer, he would like to stay on in Marsden. He knew he had grown during these years, as man and as teacher. Ah, well! 'Do the duty nearest, tho' it's dull the whiles,' " he muttered to himself.

He thought of the old town in reference to the faraway war. It had seemed so untouched by it. The great courthouse towered, gold crowned as usual, the church spires pointed heavenward, men went about their conventional tasks, on the outskirts of the community the College stood, ivy covered, serene, its general traditions still prevailing. After reading the articles that cried out to him from the magazines of the day, Gavin had once spoken seriously to Bruce.

"About drugs, now. I never see any evidence of that. You would be in a better position than I am to know what's going on. How about it?"

Bruce had looked thoughtful. "Well, I'd say maybe a little grass here and there just for the hell of it. But I'm sure no heroin. You see, Dad, that stuff just doesn't seem to go with a college like Marsden. We're small and sort of . . . conservative. The fellahs and girls come from homes a lot like our own. They aren't running away from anything like the Hippies. The fellahs I know *like* their homes and most of them like their parents. You remember Father's Day last year? The campus was just crawling with these nice-looking older men being escorted around by their sons. That gives you an idea."

"And the so-called sexual revolt?" Gavin had pursued.

Bruce had given a short laugh. "I'm no good to ask about that, for I've not been sleeping around, as you very well know. But I'd say all that is probably just about the way it's always been. Some go in for it and some don't. One thing, though, since you've evidently been reading up on it. The boys aren't allowed in the girls' rooms here nor the girls in the boys'. And a darned good thing I'd say. No use making it all harder than it is. So, all in all, I don't think you can get any really hot stuff out of Marsden. You'll have to go farther afield."

And so it had been with the war. The town was serene. There were no victory rallies as in the last war; no speeches, *no songs,* even. This latter seemed to Gavin particularly sad and significant. His mind went over the songs he and his buddies had shouted out in World War II.

"Praise the Lord and pass the ammunition."

"Accentuate the positive, eliminate the negative . . ."

And so on. Now it seemed there were no voices raised at home as the young men left. And strangely, only a relative few of them had gone. Perhaps this was the answer.

Gavin shook his head, as he pondered. And according to the Judge, there was only the incredible blind courage of the men out there upon which to hold you steady in your thinking.

He turned into the familiar drive and stopped the car under the apple tree before the garage. All seemed quiet in the house. He found Cecily perched on the kitchen stool, notebook in hand.

"Oh, Gavin!" she exclaimed. "You've been gone so long. Can I make you some lunch? You left without it, you know."

"No thanks, I'll forage. What are you up to? Where's Phoebe?"

"She's making curtains up in the sewing room, hangings, rather, for their bedroom and Cissie, her little shadow, is with her. As to me . . .''

"Yes, please, as to you."

"Well, I've been concentrating like crazy on the dinner party. For the extra couple I always want the Devereuxs but Marie is very fussy about coming here oftener than we go there, so I called Bob and he suggested the Carters. Our being there at the cocktail party makes it all right to invite them, and they are lots of fun. They're friends of Bob's, too.''

"Good enough."

"And for the extra woman—don't smile—I've asked Mrs. Wilson. Of course she's so much older, but she's so charming and she seemed very pleased to accept. Bob will call for her. He's crazy about her.''

"This seems to be Bob's party."

She did not return his smile. "Yes, it is, in a way. You know why." Her voice sounded hurt.

He was penitent at once. "I understand of course, darling, and I think it's the finest thing you could have done just now. I'm very grateful myself. Did you say black tie?"

"Well, yes, I did. I hadn't thought of it, really, until Mrs. Hastings asked, then Mrs. Carter and Bob, too. So I went ahead. It does give a little fillip to the occasion and I haven't had a formal dinner for ages. You don't mind, do you?"

"Of course not. I like to get into my monkey-suit."

"And I think I'll get Jenny Soames to help in the kitchen. Bruce and Phoebe can serve and that will leave me completely free. I want it all to be the very last word. Oh, I do hope I won't be nervous!"

But even though the children rose stoutly to her aid, and Gavin too, where he could, Cecily did feel a little tremor as it neared the time for the guests to arrive on the mild September evening of the party. The house had charm and with the skillful use of a rug over a worn spot in the carpet and a cushion over a faded corner of a slipcover, its deficiencies were hidden from sight. The curtains hung crisp and fresh and there were flowers everywhere. On the dining-room table the tall epergne (salvaged long ago from the second-hand shop and cleaned and mended with loving care) now supported a cascade of pink petunias with candles on either side to match.

"It really *is* a pretty setting," Cecily told Gavin in their room, "but please zip me up, for my hand is just a little shaky."

"You've made the setting," he said as he kissed her, "but it's not half lovely enough for you. And *please* don't be nervous. No one that's coming is worthy of that."

There were delighted outcries in regard to the house from the Hastings and Carters, who had never been there before, and a quiet expression of satisfaction from Mrs. Wilson. The dinner was superb as to food and gay as to conversation, there being no effort made to introduce a serious note. But while there was a gratified sparkle at the table, there was eventually a new pleasure evident when the bridge tables were set up. Cecily had made doubly sure that her guests were all enthusiasts for the game, and so they took their places now with willingness. Even Liz Carter, who was proverbially forgetful with a sort of harum-scarum personality, became a model of concentration when she held a hand of cards.

It proved, indeed, an unusually congenial group of players. Hour after hour passed and, still all intent, they fought the battle of the rubbers. It was after one o'clock when Cecily had to change from phenomenal luck with Bob to a series of very poor hands with Gavin as her next partner. The contrast was so striking that there were joking comments even before Liz Carter made her pronouncement. "You see, Cecily, the fates have spoken. Bob should be your life partner instead of Gavin. That would bring you luck.''

Gavin was quick. ''Now, Liz, please. I might have something to say about that. Come on, Cecily, let's show them. I open with two hearts.''

Cecily felt happy and content over Gavin's reply and turned to see what Bob to her right would bid. To her horror she saw that his face was brick-red.

''Look at Bob,'' Liz Carter was saying delightedly. ''He's blushing. I must have hit a sensitive nerve.''

''Oh, Liz, don't you know Bob always blushes when you tease him?'' Cecily put in quickly.

''No, I didn't. I never saw him . . .''

''Come on, Liz,'' her husband said, ''we're playing bridge. What are you doing about the two hearts bid, Bob?''

''Double,'' he said laconically.

''Two spades,'' Cecily returned, knowing at that moment she would have said anything.

''Game in hearts,'' Gavin ended and the playing began.

Fortunately he made it, and the guests, including Bob, settled into their usual concentration. But the dreadful moment with its inescapable significance had been there for those at one table, at least, to see, and Cecily's heart ached.

It was two o'clock when the party broke up. Even Mrs. Wilson admitted to leaving the game with reluctance. Bob had regained his usual savoir faire and was loud in his praise of everything, the dinner, the company, the bridge. "And now," he ended, "I must get this dear lady safely home," turning to Mrs. Wilson. "I think we've kept you out a bit late."

"Not at all. It's been good for me. I wish you'd come as a group for a return game with me some night."

This brought a pleasurable response in addition to all the thanks and warm comments for the evening and everything ended outwardly on a happy note until Liz Carter, who could always be counted upon to make a bad matter worse, said to Cecily along with her good-byes, "Did I really put my foot in it? I never *dreamed* that Bob had any romantic feeling . . ."

"Don't be silly, Liz. He's simply a good old friend of the family."

"But he turned red as a peony!"

Her husband took her arm firmly and

marched her off, while Cecily, with Gavin supporting her, tried to say the light and casual things to the departing guests.

When they had all left, Gavin put away the card tables and Cecily emptied ash trays and washed glasses in the kitchen. Neither spoke. At last Gavin came out and stood beside her.

"Well?" he said gently.

Cecily's sigh came from her heart. "I tried so hard, having the party to make everything natural and easy for Bob, and for us, too, and now it's all worse than we could have imagined. I'm so sad over it, Gavin. What can we do next?"

"Nothing," he said. "If Bob wants to say anything he'll come to me. As to the rest, they all know Liz and what outrageous things she always says. They will probably laugh this off and forget it. And *any* man could have felt embarrassed over her remark. I might have colored up myself if she had put me in such a spot. Let's just try to forget it. The party itself was a huge success."

The news came the next day. Bruce came in from his job, his face white.

"What's wrong, Bruce?" his father asked.

The boy dropped into a chair. "No matter

how we feel or what he did, it's bound to be a shock . . . ."

"What?"

"The word's just come. Lester Scott was killed last night driving a sports car at ninety miles an hour, I guess. And of course he couldn't know the roads there. Mr. Scott's office in Paris called up so they gave the details. It seems sort of hard to believe, Dad, in one way. He was so full of life, even though everyone knew he was running for trouble. I feel pretty shook up."

There was not much conversation at the dinner table, except Cissie's childish chatter, and afterwards the young people all left abruptly. To seek their contemporaries, Gavin thought, and with them to discuss the strange incongruity of the death of the young, the gay, the full-of-life.

Gavin and Cecily spoke little in the evening until at nine Gavin stood up.

"I think I'll have to go to see Scott, darling."

"Oh, Gavin, you *couldn't.*"

"Maybe I can't. But I feel I must make the attempt. Please don't try to dissuade me." He kissed her and went out.

He was thinking as he drove through the quiet streets of all the strange interweaving of life with life. Lester was dead, and Rose was carrying his child. Something of the old bitterness left his heart, as he considered this. On the one hand the sad finality, on the other life's vital continuance. As to Scott himself, he knew why he felt that he must see him. It was because the older man now had nothing but the empty aridity of the years ahead while Gavin himself had the rich fruition of sons and daughters. He drove on.

At the door the butler met him gravely. "Mr. Scott is seeing no one," he said.

"Will you tell him, please, that Mr. McAllister is here?"

It seemed a long time until the man returned. "He's in the library, sir, if you'll go in."

Gavin went softly over the heavy rugs, thinking of the last day he had been there. He was surprised that Scott would be willing to see him. When he reached the room he remembered, Scott was sitting in a chair beside the low fire, one trembling hand shading his eyes.

"Well, McAllister, go on, say what I suppose you've come to say. I guess I deserve it." His tone was tense.

"I came," Gavin said, "to offer you my very deepest sympathy."

"That was all?"

"That was all."

For several minutes there was silence, with Scott drawing heavy breaths as though to release the depths of his misery.

"I thought," he said at last, "that you had come to tell me that retribution had fallen upon me and my . . . house."

"Not at all," Gavin answered. "I do not believe in a retributive God."

"Will you sit down?" Scott asked suddenly. "People have been here, everybody and his brother and the preachers, worst of all. I am too weary to listen any longer to talk but I would like to know somebody is near. Could you just sit there and keep quiet?"

"Of course," Gavin answered.

"And you say you don't believe in retribution from God?"

"I do not."

There was a long sigh. And the quiet began. Scott leaned his head against the back of the chair and closed his eyes. Gavin sat, strangely relaxed, opposite him. He watched the furnishings of the room. On the mantel a little ormolu clock was ticking with a soft staccato haste. On either side of it were animals which he guessed had belonged to

Lester in his boyhood and were placed here for safekeeping: a deer and a really beautiful lamb which looked as though it were made of marble. There was something touching to Gavin in these decorations in a man's library. The father's heart apparently still yearned over his son's boyhood. There were pictures of Lester at all ages and several of a very beautiful woman, evidently his mother, the largest an oil above the mantel. If she had lived, Gavin thought, this night of sorrow might not have come to pass. Who could know?

The little clock ticked on to strike nine, then ten, and moved toward eleven. Gavin was growing anxious. Was Scott asleep? If so, should he waken him? At least the long, hard racking breaths had stopped and as the little clock struck eleven Scott roused himself.

"I shouldn't have kept you so long, McAllister, but you've rendered me a great service which I won't soon forget. Thank you for coming."

He rose and hesitantly held out his hand. Gavin took it in his own. "If there is anything else I can do . . ." he said.

"I don't see how you are able to do anything in view of all that's past. I know more than you realize."

Gavin hesitated. The word *empathy* came again to his mind. Surely it applied now.

"In the face of sorrow such as yours, Mr. Scott, other troubles seem smaller. I hope you are able to sleep tonight."

When he reached home, Cecily was waiting up. They talked briefly and then Gavin said he felt they should write at once to Rose. "She'll get the word somehow, and I think it should come from us."

"You write then, Gavin."

He sat down at the desk and felt the burden a hard one.

MY DEAR CHILD: [he wrote at last]

A tragic piece of news has just come to town, concerning Lester Scott. He was driving at great speed along a dangerous road in France, and the car went out of control. While everyone has expected him to meet with an accident, the fact that this was a fatal one has of course been a shock to both young and old. One reason I am writing is that I hope you will never feel that God, Whoever or What-ever he may be, brought this disaster upon Lester because of the mistakes of his life. He was, as we know, a selfish, headstrong, disobedient boy, and *indirectly* these qualities did bring about his death. But the immediate cause was that he was driving too fast around a sharp curve. Try always to understand this, dear, and never feel that God was bringing a direct retribution upon him. I do not feel God works in that way.

I hope you will share this letter with Abe, and then try to forget all the story, for this is the end of the chapter. We are all well and your mother will be writing soon.

Love always,
DADDY

There was a strange quiet in the town for the next few days, especially among the young people, as though some vital, life-abounding nerve had been severed. Even while in France Lester had constantly written, cabled, even telephoned to his friends, expense to him being no consideration. His delight in the gay life he was leading had come through by various media to the sober streets of Marsden. Now, the light-hearted voice was still.

Cecily had gone at once to see Mrs. Wilson. Her patrician features were white and strained. "I feel sure," she said, "that I could have done more to guide him, to restrain him. I have a weight on my heart."

"Please try not to feel so," Cecily said. "I think he was like a young colt that could not be tamed. You did give him love and all the advice you could. No one, certainly no woman, could have done more." She felt a great affection for her older friend as she watched her, burdened with remorse. She reached up and kissed her gently. "There are so many kinds of sorrow, but somehow we are able to bear them all."

Mrs. Wilson rested her cheek against Cecily's rounded one. "Thank you," she said. "You are much braver than I."

I'm sure she knows, Cecily thought as she went back home.

The crickets chirred in the evening grasses, the cicadas were vocal by day, all the good old-fashioned housewives made jelly and all the girls, little and big, wore brave bright dresses for the first day of school. Even the boys tried to look unaware of their new plaid jackets. Gavin collected his notebooks that morning, ate the unusually good breakfast Cecily had prepared for him, and started off down the street with a leaden heart. A second good if small thing about the new situation was that he could walk to his work. This, at least, he would enjoy.

He went into the large vestibule, his nostrils dilating with distaste, but he tried to put on a bravely casual front when he stopped in Hastings' office.

"I've done the very best I could in the matter of arranging your periods," the latter said, a small pucker showing between his brows. "In order to assure you both the Junior and Senior English classes I've had to give you the first study period with the Freshman boys. I hope you won't mind too much."

Gavin smiled. "Why, of course not. That will give me a chance to look over some of the work I want to use later."

"If you have any problems, please let me know," Hastings said earnestly.

Gavin had difficulty in restraining a laugh, though his feelings were rather hurt. What does he suppose I am, he thought, a brand-new graduate from Normal School?

He went on upstairs to the room for study period, laid out some papers on the desk and waited for the gong to ring. When it did, the boys, thirty strong, who had evidently been waiting outside in the halls somewhere, came in together like a herd of young cattle. Books fell and were picked up, bodies pushed each other, muffled exclamations were numerous. Gavin rapped smartly on his desk with a ruler.

"Be seated, please, as quickly as possible."

There was then a sudden rush for the seats into which the boys seemed to collapse. It was quite apparent that they were bent upon testing the new teacher's nerves by all means in their power. Gavin stood before them, confident in his age, experience and manly strength.

"I realize," he said, "that this is not only the first day of school but also for you all the first day in High School. You have now crossed the line that separates little boys from big boys. I expect you now to behave like young gentlemen. Tomorrow morning you will please come in quietly, go to your seats, which will now be given to you in alphabetical order, and begin your studies."

He began then to take the roll and assign the seats. Underneath a nominal silence, there were the peculiar vibrations of a steady unrest. By the time he had finished the roll Gavin felt hot and perspiring. He stood before them again and with a friendly smile pointed to the blackboard upon which the teacher of the next period had written some simple exercises.

"Now," he added, "we'll all get to work."

There followed then the most subtle form of torture known to a teacher. With faces of bland innocence the thirty boys stared at Gavin and the blackboard alternately while a pencil dropped, a book fell, a shoe scraped, a queer ventriloquistic sound came from an undefinable spot. When the gong sounded, Gavin, feeling weak in the pit of his stomach, stood at the door and saw to it that at least they made their exit quietly. The rest of the day went so pleasantly that he was inclined to forget the first study period, and if he thought of it at all, to set it down to "first day" mischief.

But as the weeks went on he had to revise his thinking. That study hall of Freshman boys was wearing him down. Instead of mastering the problem he felt less and less confident. The matter of discipline had never entered into his teaching before. In the present situation he felt that some dynamic force in himself was lacking. No teacher was allowed to lay physical hands on a boy, the principal only being permitted that privilege.

If, Gavin thought, each morning he could pick two young recalcitrants up and bump their heads together, how simple it would be! But rather than humiliate himself by confessing to Hastings that he was having real trouble, he would somehow put up with it. He tried many devices, but none of them worked. The boys grew more ingenious in their subtle deviltry, and Gavin grew more and more tired-looking at the end of the day, even though his English classes were shaping up better than he had hoped.

One night Bruce tapped on the study door. "It's me, Dad."

"Well, come in. How's college going?"

"Fine. Outside of missing you, I'm enjoying my courses more than ever. Phoebe is too. There's something I'd like to ask you. You've always had an uncanny way of knowing when something's wrong with me. Now, maybe it's presumptuous of me but I feel *you're* worried about something. Could you tell me?"

Gavin looked into his son's fine, solicitous gray eyes and a sudden desire overtook him to share his burden. "I *am* worried," he admitted, "and I believe I'll tell you the whole problem."

When he had finished, Bruce gave vent to

a few expletives, which soothed Gavin's spirit, and then sat on the edge of the desk and brooded upon the matter. "The trouble, Dad, is that you're just too mature for those damned kids. As you say you don't dare knock one of them down or thrash him. But that's not your pitch anyway. What they need is someone . . ."

He was thoughtful for a minute and then got up. "Don't worry," he said. "A situation like this is sure to be ironed out. Just relax, and take it easy."

Two days later, when the study hall was settling into its usual state of disquietude, there was a light knock on the door and through it came John Partridge looking several inches taller and much wider than Gavin remembered him at their last strange conference. Behind him were two other boys only slightly smaller.

"Hello, Professor," John began. "We were just passing and thought we'd drop in and say hello."

"Why, John!" Gavin exclaimed with real pleasure. "This is very nice of you. I'm awfully glad to see you!"

"You remember Harkins and Post, don't you? They're Juniors this year, but they're mighty good on the team."

"Of course," Gavin said, shaking hands with the other two giants. "Well, how is everything going?"

"Not so good in some ways," John said. "We miss you at College, Professor. I hope," he added, glancing over the room, "that the students here know what they've got. By the way, how are these kids here behaving themselves, Professor?"

There was a silence that could be felt. Not one of the thirty, now raising worshipful eyes to their god, but had at the College games yelled, "Yea Partridge! Go it Partridge! *Yea Partridge!*"

"How're they behavin' themselves, Professor?" John repeated in the dead quiet.

"Well, now, I'll tell you, John. I would say that in another year or so these boys are going to be fine fellows."

"Take a little time, eh? Well, I just want to say that if any of them get out of line or give you any trouble all you've got to do is to tip the wink to me and we'll attend to it. Be a pleasure. Wouldn't it, fellows?"

"Sure would," the other giants concurred solemnly, sweeping the room with their eyes.

"Well, we've got to get on, but it's good to see you, Professor. And don't forget what I told you. As a matter of fact . . ." John studied the hushed faces before him, "there might be some good football material here after a while. Scrub team, you know. Well, good-bye now, and take it easy, Professor."

Gavin's good-byes and thanks were heart-felt. While at first his lips had twitched in amusement over his callers they felt now more like trembling. He walked back to his desk and sat down for once to his papers in utter stillness, which lasted until the close of the period. And day after day it continued. After weeks of this new freedom, Gavin began to chat with the boys and they in turn made shy overtures of friendship toward him. He could see them from the moment of John Partridge's call eyeing him with new respect. Some of the golden dust of their god had brushed off on his coat, he thought, smiling. Now, he could get close to them.

Bruce, when told of it, was casual about the Partridge visit. "Oh, he thinks you're the *most,* Dad," he said. "Well, it was nice of him to stop in."

Gavin laughed. "You may be interested to know that my problem is solved," he said, "and that aside from being a good son, you're a good *friend.* So, thanks."

"I don't know what you're talking about exactly but it all sounds good to me, especially about the problem. You really *do* look better.''

As the autumn weeks flowed on the family settled into an even routine. Cecily found a number of party invitations coming in, the acceptance of which she insisted to Gavin was good for them both. Bob, when they saw him, was his usual self as though no embarrassing moment had occurred. Phoebe helped Ian with his French in which she was quite proficient, Bruce worked late hoping for his fellowship at the end of the year. Even little Cissie seemed to have developed a taste, at last, for books. And Gavin found himself, if not buoyantly happy in his work as he had once been, at least content.

The letters from Rose were coming more often and while giving no reason for it, seemed to convey a little extra warmth. Her parents read them over and over, pondering.

In late October Gavin came home one afternoon to find Cecily in a state of mild hysteria, though it seemed from happiness rather than pain. She flung herself at her husband, telling her news with difficulty.

"Gavin, you'd never *never* guess . . . you simply couldn't imagine what's happened! I would never have believed it. It's simply . . .''

"Now just please calm yourself, darling, and tell me what this is all about."

"B-Bunny's going to have a baby! Now if there's any bigger news than that, I'd like to hear it. Don't you think it's wonderful?"

"I do, indeed. How did you hear?"

"Well, she told Marie Devereux first because of course Marie's responsible for the whole thing."

"Oh come now. Give Schneider a *little* credit."

"Gavin, you're dreadful. I mean Marie brought them together and really made the match. Oh, I am so pleased for them. Marie says that Dev says that Bunny will teach only until they find a substitute and meanwhile Schneider runs down to her room between classes to make sure she's all right." Cecily giggled. "I think I'll go over tonight to see her and I'll start at once knitting a baby blanket. Why haven't you said more, Gavin?"

"For one thing because you've given me no time, but I'll say now I think it's terrific!"

He started up the stairs, chuckling to himself. "So old Schneider was *adequate* after all."

"What did you say, Gavin?" Cecily called after him.

"Oh, just another comment on the great news," he said.

Indian summer was short that year. October's gold and November's magnificence of color were both early lost in chill, driving rains. The leaves lay prostrate on the pavements and the trees were too soon bare. By Thanksgiving small showers of snow had begun and the old inhabitants prophesied a hard winter ahead. Gavin worked hard on the Saturdays in which it was possible, putting his garden to sleep for the winter, while indoors Cecily with Phoebe's help took down the summer's cool, ruffled curtains and put up the warm-hued hangings at the windows. There was a sort of between-season hush as nature and men girded themselves for the coming onslaught of cold. There was a hush also in the hearts of Gavin and Cecily as they waited for the postman.

Rose had written first that the doctor thought the baby would be born late in December. He had decided now it would be early in January. Either time was coming nearer.

While Cecily had the busy routine of her house and family and the social activities that seemed to multiply with the weeks to dull a little of the ache in her heart for Rose, Gavin in addition to family and work had a new anxiety that haunted him. He had dropped in to see Billy King one evening after school and was appalled. Just during the short time since he had been there before he found Billy wretchedly changed, thin, dejected and coughing hard. Without waiting for discussion he had gone out at once for young Seely, the new doctor lately come to town who he felt might be willing to compromise with Billy's needs and peculiarities, briefing him as speedily as possible on the way back. He brought the young man into the drab apartment and introduced him, then drew a sigh of relief, for the doctor leaned back in his chair with no attempt at examination. Instead he remarked that he had heard somewhere that Mr. King had once spent some time in Paris. Oddly enough he had, himself, during his Junior year in college. It seemed as though so few people were interested in Paris . . . For a short time the Left Bank seemed to be at the edge of the room.

It was after quite a while that Dr. Seely came down to professional business. "Sort of a cough you have there. I think I can give you some medicine to help that. No objection to taking a small amount of whiskey as a chaser, have you?''

Billy raised himself up in his chair. "For the love of the Lord," he said, his eyes glistening with pleasure, "you're the first doctor I ever met that had a grain of common sense. Go ahead if you want to, and look me over. I think I can trust you for the rest after that. As a matter of fact I may not be in too good shape."

Dr. Seely with this sanction went about his skillful work. When he had finished Billy spoke blithely.

"Well, what's the prognosis?"

"Why, I would say a week in bed with some pretty nice things to eat would do wonders for you. Oh, Mr. King, what wouldn't we give for a good French *bonne!* But maybe I can scare up somebody who can make good soup anyway."

Gavin spoke up. "I'll help Mr. King to bed and see he has some supper."

"Good," said the doctor. "I'll pop in now and then for another chat. Nice to have met you, Mr. King."

When he was gone Gavin set to work tidying the room and then getting Billy to bed. There were some good canned soups on the shelves, and with this and toast he had all

Billy needed for the night. He would get Cecily to make some light desserts tomorrow. When he called up the doctor later, though, he was shocked.

"I'm afraid your old friend's in a bad way, Mr. McAllister. He's on the very edge of pneumonia and his resistance is nil. I've located a good woman who will come in each day and look after him. But I'd say it's touch and go. We'll try to cut down the whiskey by using it after the medicine. I'll go in again soon. I like the old chap."

"You mean it's quite serious?"

"Very."

"I'll keep a close watch and thank you for the way you approached him. He likes you enormously and this may be as important as the medicine in his case. He can be quite wild if his drinking habits are interfered with."

"We can't take the stuff away altogether, but if we ration it this way it may work. We can try. Is he a relative, Mr. McAllister?"

"None whatever. I've just been fond of the old man."

"Has he any relatives who should know of his condition?"

"I'm afraid none at all. You might be interested in his story sometime."

"I would. And I'll look in on him again tomorrow."

Gavin called Bob at once to let him know the facts and find out how the expenses could be handled.

"I think we can manage," Bob said. "I'm his lawyer, you know. That has its funny side, but it's a help. I once got him to give me power of attorney so I can handle his checks as they come in. I've often done so in any case since he has stopped his trips uptown, and I've managed to save quite a little. Just let me know what's needed. I'll run in to see him myself tomorrow."

As often happens with the old and weak, the bed, freshly made, felt good to Billy and he decided to spend a few days there until his strength returned, not knowing, of course, that he would never be out of it. When Gavin went in the next day he found the practical nurse already installed. Billy beckoned him to the bedroom and with carefully lowered voice between coughing and chuckles gave his report.

"As heaven is my witness, that she-male out there looks like Aunt Bessie! It's uncanny, but somehow I like it."

He grew weaker day by day and lay content in the main until the evenings closed in with their steady stillicide of rain. Then he became restless and asked constantly for Gavin.

"I think, darling," Gavin said to his wife, "I'll have to plan to sit with him into the nights a little. Until he falls asleep, you know. The doctor says it may not be too long."

"You'll grow so tired after teaching all day."

"I'm strong. I can stand it. Poor old Billy. I'll miss him when he's gone. This is not much to do for him. You understand?"

"Of course. It's just that you're wearing yourself out. Do leave as soon as you can."

But this was not always early, for Billy napped occasionally during the day and then brightened a little when Gavin arrived. The doctor had found another woman who, although she had no nursing qualifications, would stay at least on guard during the night. Billy needed little care and strangely enough his "chasers" after the medicine seemed to satisfy him. Even the demanding taste for liquor had left him.

He usually began on poetry when his old friend was beside him. "Let's have 'Dover Beach,' Gavin," or perhaps, "What about old Omar? I feel in the mood especially for the last part of that, only there's no moon with all this damned rain."

Sometimes his mind wandered vaguely between Paris and New York and occasionally, while half asleep, he would chuckle, "Aunt Bessie's Tom cat."

Gavin read to him, recited much from memory and listened to the labored accounts of Billy's younger years. Often when he was sure the patient was asleep he would try gently to disengage his hand to which Billy always clung. But this was rarely successful. "I feel better when you're here," Billy would say, starting up. "Please stay a little longer."

So night after night Gavin kept his vigil, praying that he could stay awake and conscientiously alert the next day. But there came an evening in which the doctor returned after his office hours and Gavin himself knew as soon as he arrived earlier that Billy's frail hold on life was lessening rapidly. He had felt it the night before when Billy had surprised him by asking for Browning's "Prospice." He had read the last lines, wondering.

"Then a light, then thy breast,
  O thou soul of my soul! I shall clasp thee
    again!
And with God be the rest!"

When he finished Billy whispered, brokenly, "I was in love once. Never got over it." And then spoke no more, at all.

When the pitifully bare and sad ceremonials decreed by custom were over on Saturday morning, Bob asked Gavin to come with him to Billy's apartment. "I know this is hard for you, but Billy specially asked for it." So they went back together and Bob explained.

"Billy was most anxious that everything should be meticulously correct, even to my reading of his will here after the burial. He said that was the way it was always done."

"His *will?*" Gavin said, startled.

"Yes, a number of years ago he made one. It's touching since as you know he has nothing to will except the furnishings of this apartment, but he insisted it must be drawn up with my most legal ability. You, as you might guess, are his sole legatee."

"Oh, my God!" said Gavin. "Poor Billy. I wish I had done more for him."

"You certainly did enough."

"Nothing you do is ever enough. Go ahead if you have to read that. It touches me so, I can hardly stand it."

"I'll go over it quickly except for the lines

To my beloved friend, Professor Gavin McAllister, I bequeath everything of which I may die possessed. The rest is just the usual legal verbiage. Well, Gavin, you can have the pictures you've often admired and the shelf of books. I'm sure there's nothing else of value in the rooms. All the rest of his remittances have had to be used."

"We can let Gertie, the cleaning woman, come in and have what she wants. Of course I'll take the books and the pictures. Would you want one of the paintings, Bob?"

"No, no. They are definitely yours. Why don't you take them now and the books, too, then you needn't come back."

They carried them out and put them in the car, and Gavin drove home with a sense of mortality pressing heavily upon him. Once there he and Cecily hung the paintings in places of honor on the walls. With gentle cleaning of one corner Gavin found Billy's initials as he had supposed on his favorite picture. He stood long, looking at it; *Les Bouquinistes* with Notre Dame in a soft mist in the background.

"What talent!" he kept repeating. "And what sad waste of a life."

He put the books up reverently in the center of the shelves where in a sense they could dominate the family scene.

It was Saturday morning, several weeks later, when Bob called up.

"Gavin, could you come down to the office for a few minutes soon? There is something I have to talk over with you."

Gavin felt an instant pang. This was it, he thought. This was what he had instinctively feared. This would be the unspeakably sad talk between two men, friends of each other, who loved the same woman. He was the more certain of this because the night before the group that they had entertained for dinner and bridge were at Mrs. Wilson's. It had been a delightful evening without a single faux pas from Liz Carter. But as he watched his wife, Gavin thought he had never seen her look lovelier. She was less animated than usual, her thoughts being so much with Rose, but the red dress she wore sent a rich color to her cheeks, and her bright smile and flashes of wit still came at intervals. She had, without effort, held on to youth and the desirability that went with it.

She was out at a neighbor's fortunately at the moment, so Gavin got into the car and drove off to Main Street where Bob had his office in one of the bank buildings. He parked, then climbed the shabby stairs heavily, the odor of dust and old tobacco surrounding him. For even eminent jurists through the years had pursued their weighty legal matters in comfortable offices with small concern for the approach leading to them. An old Marsden habit.

Gavin tapped on Bob's door and then opened it slowly, his heart beating fast. But Bob rose to greet him, not with a stricken face but with a countenance positively glowing.

"Sit down, Gavin. Maybe you can't take this standing up. You've had some rough breaks this year but now, by the beard of the prophet, I've got some good news for you!"

"What in the world do you mean?"

"Well, I'll admit it's a queer deal, but it's as legal as the Constitution. When Billy died I wrote the New York bank to apprise them of the fact so that his monthly remittance could be stopped. Meanwhile I had the will probated, of course. The bank replied that long years ago the sum of $25,000 had been deposited under the name of William Ellison King by his aunt, Miss Bessie. She stated that she did not wish her nephew to know of the existence of this deposit then as he was not capable of handling money wisely. She would tell him later on when she saw fit.

Since his own checking account was in the name of W. E. King, there would be no confusion."

Bob paused to open an envelope. "What evidently happened as the years went on was that Aunt Bessie with all her art and theater and *cat* interests simply forgot about it! The bank asked for a copy of the will and since, fortunately, in it Billy had used his full name in all his signatures, the whole thing is clear as day. This check arrived this morning and as Billy's executor I now happily pass it over to you."

Gavin looked up in distress. "But this seems dreadful. If Billy had only known of it he could have had it to enjoy, himself."

"Not at all," said Bob firmly. "If he had had the money he would have spent the most of it over the years on drink as you very well know. Now it will be put to good use. Take it, man. It's yours by legal and moral right. Why, Gavin, don't let this *throw* you!"

For Gavin's hand that picked up the check shook and there were tears in his eyes.

"I've stood up to a good many hard things this last year, but a sudden piece of good fortune like this is enough to kill me."

Bob brought a bottle and glasses from the shelves. "Here," he said, "you need a bracer, and I think I can do with one myself. I'm about as shook-up over this as you are. What will you do with the money? Your Doctorate?''

"Of course. But I'll have to finish out this year first. I can't let Hastings down. He's been too good to me.''

They parted at last, with Gavin's eyes still misty and his voice unsteady as he spoke his thanks to Bob.

"You'll have a nice surprise for Cecily,'' the latter said gently. "And watch where you're going—down these stairs. You must get back in one piece with your news.''

Gavin drove home very slowly. It was as though he wanted to hug to himself the wonderful, the incredible beneficence that had befallen him, without words to mar the miracle. Only for a time, of course, for there would come soon the joy of sharing it with Cecily and then the family. But for just a little longer . . . He drove past the entrance to Marsden College, and for the first time felt no hurt; he drove past the Judge's house, but that happy conversation could wait; once he cautiously felt in his pocket for the check. It was there. It was real.

He drove out to the country lane where he had parked that afternoon after he had resigned his professorship. Here too, strangely, he found the bitterness gone. Then he drove quickly back home. As he parked under the familiar apple tree his lips moved: "In so far as it lies in my power I'll see to it, Billy, that your life shall not be wasted, after all."

Eight

BY MEANS OF the peculiar news osmosis which prevails especially in towns where the inhabitants have long known each other, it was less than a week until the fact of Gavin's inheritance was common knowledge. As he walked along the street, friends, neighbors, acquaintances made bold to stop him and mention his good fortune, at first tentatively, and then with more assurance, as Gavin made no attempt to disguise his pleasure. One remark often made was, "It came as a shock to me that Billy King was a man of any substance whatever."

"He was an odd man, in many ways," Gavin always said, "but a cultured and interesting person, and my very good friend. I shall miss him."

Then, having replied so, Gavin thought to himself, if Billy receives a little good notoriety from all this I will be doubly glad.

The strangest conversation by far was one with Loren Scott. The two men met as they emerged from the paper store one late afternoon and, as Scott directed, walked along together. The older man had accepted his great sorrow with courage and was attempting, apparently, to renew the other interests of his life. Already it was said he was arranging to enlarge his coke and coal holdings. After a few moments of silence now, he spoke.

"I hear you have had quite a pleasant windfall, McAllister."

"Yes," Gavin answered. "I have."

"I think it was Bob St. Clair who intimated you were thinking of spending this money in study for your Doctorate."

"Yes, that is my intention."

"Very commendable," said Scott. "That will open up for you a much wider range of positions in the future. There are always changes. Older men grow older, younger ones take their places. Now we as trustees, for example, are seeing the first part of that statement fulfilled now. In only one more year after this one, Waring will have reached retirement age and will resign as president here. The trustees then will want to secure a younger man of initiative and unimpeachable

308

integrity, I may say, who would get on well with both students and faculty. Yes, there are always changes, but that's what makes the world go round. Very interested to hear of your good fortune, McAllister."

And he turned down toward his own street, leaving Gavin with strange pricklings up and down his spine which he managed to control. Scott's words were nothing, and yet they were something. Something to take out and look at in the silence of the night.

Except for the constant thought of Rose the weeks before Christmas were happy ones. In Gavin's heart a heavy dull weight of indefinite disappointment had been lifted. In its place was the warm security of ambition possible of achievement, and hope, not deferred, but preciously within the grasp.

Cecily was radiant over her husband's happiness and tried to share with him his sudden feeling that all the news from Rose would be good. Letters and packages had been flying back and forth across the sea for a month, and now with the unusually large bank account, real gifts in their bright wrappings began to be smuggled in and hidden carefully against the day itself. As for the dinner, Cecily talked earnestly with Gavin.

"Bob has had Christmas dinner here for years on end. We *couldn't* not invite him this year, could we?"

"Certainly not. This year above all others. Would we ask anyone else who has no kinfolk to make what you call a 'full table'?"

Cecily shook her head. "I'm a coward, I suppose, and I shouldn't hesitate, but my heart is still anxious and it makes me tired all over. Let's just have the family and Bob. The Judge will be going to his nephew's as usual, so he's taken care of. Having Phoebe here will be a great help in every way, and there will be all the good fortune to discuss. But I don't feel up to a big dinner party. I'm just too tired," she repeated.

He held her close and spoke reassuring words. "The thing is that after you've been brave for a long time and the tension is suddenly released, it leaves you rather limp. We've both felt that about the position and the money. Now, very soon, I'm sure we're going to feel it about Rose. But say, I suddenly have a thought."

It was that while the family and Bob would dine quietly as now planned, it might be nice to invite a few, otherwise alone, to come in perhaps at five for some of Cecily's famous mulled cider.

"That would be no strain and no trouble, really, and might be good for everybody. What do you think?" he asked eagerly.

"I think it would be wonderful! I'll tell Phoebe and let her sort of take charge of this part. She and Bruce can be the hosts, as it were, and that will insure their being here and Ian too. I feel better already. Something pleasant but no trouble to plan for."

As a matter of fact Phoebe's attitude toward the preparations was touching in the extreme to the McAllisters. It developed that her father had not approved of holiday celebrations so now as she baked star cookies, blanched almonds, carefully dropped a bit more brandy on the fruit cake, spiced the cider and decorated the house with greens, she went about in a trance of delight. Once she put her arms about Cecily and laid her cheek against that of her mother-in-law.

"I'm so happy here," she whispered.

It was plain that Bruce, too, was quietly elated over the idea of playing host with Phoebe, so the five o'clock plans went forward. The Schneiders were quite alone, the Devereuxs also since their son was taking a college vacation tour. They all accepted eagerly.

"Would we dare ask Mrs. Wilson?" Cecily wondered.

"Let's do," said Bruce. "She always seems the same age as anybody else, and she's been sweet to Phoebe and me."

"You call her up then, Bruce. She would like that. And if she accepts I think we have enough guests. We want to feel cozy and intimate, around the fire."

Mrs. Wilson accepted with a definite catch in her throat. "The late afternoon of Christmas day," she told Bruce, "is always a little sad when you live alone. Now you are going to make it the brightest part. Thank you, my dear."

It snowed on Christmas Eve just as all true children of every age hope for. Soft feathers began in the early evening and grew to larger and larger flakes. In the morning the usual signs of streets and walks were obliterated. A temporary hush brooded over the town, but lightly as though knowing that its stay would be short and that the busy, active sons of men would not rest long beneath its gentle benison. Sounds of growling snowplows, shouts of small boys armed with brooms and shovels were soon heard and the jingle of sleighbells for which everyone awaited each snowfall as Dave Baer, an eccentric old farmer who lived on the edge of town, drove proudly through the unbroken streets with his ancient work-horse and shaky sled but immortal chiming bells. This always set the true nostalgic seal upon the winter for the older people and brought a new and pleasant tradition to the young.

"It snows!" cries the school boy,
"Hurrah! What fun!"

Gavin chanted through the upper hall. Ian poked his head around the door.

"Yes, all very well for you to say. You don't have to make the walks."

"Right. I was wise enough to provide myself with two good shovelers. Merry Christmas, everybody! Dave Baer's going by already."

"Oh, we mustn't miss the sleighbells," Cecily called. "Hurry, Cissie, put on your wrapper and come to the front so you can hear them. Merry Christmas, everyone!"

By mid-morning the driveway was open and a clean, wide walk led from the front door to the street. This was particularly comforting to Schneider who had called several times to make sure of Bunny's safe progress from car to house. And then at noon something like a vital pulse ran from room to room. It was a cable in reply to their own. It read: *Merry Christmas. Love to all* and was signed simply, *Rose.*

'As of the moment she's safe and well,'' Cecily said to her husband, ''so now let's enjoy our day as much as we can.''

It went its time-honored course. Bob arrived, armed with gifts as usual and champagne for the feast. There was quiet relaxation on the part of the older three while the young people kept a pleasant stir with jokes and laughter. The trimming of the tree the night before had been a hard hour for Cecily, for this had always been Rose's special delight. But here again Phoebe's pleasure had helped assuage the other pain.

"This is the best Christmas I've ever had," Bruce announced over the flaming pudding, "and if you all rack your brains you can maybe guess why," he added as he kissed his bride.

It's better to be alone, Cecily thought, for now there's no constraint. For at the moment, she even forgot the problem of Bob, his naturalness fitted in so well with the family's interests. She read the cable aloud for the third time.

"Just so we feel Rose is very close," she explained.

The young people took over the clearing up, after dinner, and then busied themselves earnestly with setting out the proper plates and glasses for the later guests. Gavin and Bob carried more logs and made up the fire and when at winter sunset they all sat before it there was a vast spirit of contentment evident. With the carols, which Cecily always insisted upon, came a surprise. Never before had any of them heard Schneider's magnificent bass as it rolled out now as a rich counterpoint to the higher voices.

"Why, man alive," Gavin cried as they finished the first song. "None of us knew you could sing! Why have you kept it a secret?"

Schneider was embarrassed. "I never did so. I just had no occasion to sing except in my own little laboratory. Then I let myself go."

"But it's going to be different from now on," Bunny put in. "We're getting a piano and I'm going to practice up to accompany him. Oh," she added, in a tone quite different from her usual class comments on the dead languages, "it's going to be such fun!"

The young folks plied the guests with the seasonal cakes and mulled cider and themselves joined their voices betweentimes in the old carols. The music filled the rooms, the logs burned brightly, the tree twinkled, the fragrance of the pine drifted gently, hearts and bodies relaxed, and all at once it was a happy and satisfying Christmas.

Schneider took Bunny home early, and Bob insisted on making sure Mrs. Wilson left before she was overtired. Her thanks were very tender. It was plain the simple afternoon had meant much to her. The young folks, after pleading hunger, repaired it hastily in the kitchen and were off to finish the day in their own way. There were left then at last, after Cissie was in bed, just the Devereuxs with Gavin and Cecily before the fire.

"This is the best end of the party," Marie said calmly, "when the other guests have gone and we can talk about them comfortably."

There was, as a matter of fact, much food for conversation and they all made the most of it: Schneider's voice; Bunny's enceinte condition; Mrs. Wilson's charm; the tragedy of Lester Scott once more recounted.

"Oh, Gavin, here is something I've been

wanting to ask you. Since when has Loren Scott taken such a shine to you?'' Devereux inquired.

"To *me?*" Gavin asked. "What are you talking about?"

"Well," Devereux went on, "I worked late one day last week, and I was walking along the upper hall minding my own business when I passed Waring's office and his door was open. I couldn't help hearing Scott's voice. He was saying, 'The worst thing you ever did was to let McAllister go. But as far as he's concerned I've an idea he'll end a good deal higher up than if you'd kept him.' I didn't hear any more but I wondered what had hit Scott in his solar plexus. I thought he was sort of *agin* you. He must have heard about that voting business for Lester's graduation, don't you think?"

"Oh, he probably did."

"If he had only been conversant with the Bard of Avon he could have put it so neatly:

Those Professors thou hast and their efficiency proved,
Grapple them to thy faculty with hoops of steel,
(or possibly larger salaries).''

317

The women were laughing and in the general mirth Gavin found it easy to pass over the remark casually.

"Oh, who would know what Loren Scott was thinking? But you see he just may have forgiven me now. Blessings brighten, you know . . . Can I give you some more cider, Dev?"

It was well into the evening when Gavin and Cecily were at last by themselves. "It has been a happy day in spite of everything, hasn't it?" she said. "Didn't the boys and Phoebe do well with their hosting, and wasn't Cissie adorable as she passed the cookies? You know I believe she's going to be even prettier than Rose when she grows up."

"She's very likely to be, for she looks exactly like you."

Cecily smiled, but her eyes were misty. "Don't make me pretty speeches tonight, dear, for I might cry. I'm still nervous and tired. If you don't mind, I think I'll go to bed right away."

"The best idea. I'll come up and tuck you in and say good-night, then I think I'll take a walk. I always like to get an early sight and breath of the snow before too many people have gobbled it up, so to speak."

When he did start out later he went slowly, very slowly, along the white bordered walks. The stars were shining overhead with a golden intensity, and now as in the early morning a quiet rested on the town. He wanted to be alone, to think of a possibility once and once only before pushing it completely aside in the farthest corner of his mind. In a sense it would be as cowardly of him to refuse to face this idea as it would be foolish to dwell upon it. But the thought had been planted, so he must try calmly to consider it. Loren Scott's significant speech to him on the street coupled with the remark overheard by Devereux could mean only one thing: Scott, looking far ahead as he always did, was considering *him* as a future president of Marsden! Incredible, yet Scott did not speak lightly. A warmth crept through Gavin's body, a strange pervasive sense of well-being, even though there was in it an alien quality, as though it belonged to another man. If he could in an ambitious moment choose his ultimate work, this would be it. He knew his own capacity, first as a teacher, but also as an administrator, as a man who could smoothly bring the right innovations to pass. He had a gift already proven for getting on well with both students and faculty. All this and more, without vanity, he knew.

He loved the old college; he had often yearned for its growth and advancement. If it should ever happen that he had the chance to bring this about he would consider it his life's richest fulfillment. But his native Scottish caution warned him that he had now gone far enough into the future in his thinking. A hundred different turns of fate could convert this nebulous possibility into less than a dream. The idea must be pushed back into the inner recesses of his mind, and never again as the months passed be regarded.

He smiled to himself. Only now for these few moments he could look at it, ponder it, warm his heart by it, here in the snow, under the stars, on this Christmas night.

The letter came the second week of January, addressed in Abe's small, firm hand. Fortunately it was a Saturday morning and the children were all out, for Cecily was trembling as Gavin drew her down to the couch beside him. "Steady, darling," he kept saying, "this is sure to be the good news we've been waiting for."

"You open it," she said, "and I'll shut my

eyes while you read. I have what is known as a *boding* heart."

"I'll hurry," he said, "and set your mind at rest." He opened the envelope and drew out the letter while he held his arm firmly around her.

DEAR MR. AND MRS. MCALLISTER:
First of all I must tell you that Rose is safe and gaining strength every day. She went through a very hard time, but the doctor says in another two weeks she will be almost back to normal. This is the good news and of course by far the most important. But there is some sad news also. That is that the little baby did not live. The doctors gave me the medical term for what happened but I was so upset at the time I didn't quite get it. Maybe you will know, Mrs. McAllister. Rose was very sick and for a while in danger herself and due to her condition the baby's oxygen supply was cut off. It was a beautiful little girl that looked exactly like Rose.

We are all very sad about this and poor Miss Het is inconsolable. She had counted so on having the baby to take care of. There are many things I know

Rose will want to tell you but just now while, as I said, she is safe, she is still not too strong. I discovered that during the last weeks when she couldn't go about much, she had kept a diary so I have urged her to send that on to you, and write a letter later on. This she has agreed to do, so I'm mailing it now and you should receive it in a few days. I wish the news could all have been good, but the wonderful part is that Rose is safe and getting well. I'll write often and I know she will look for your letters now more than ever.

Love,
ABE

Cecily gave a long shuddering breath. "So I *was* right. My heart told me she was in danger. Oh, I should have gone over and been with her. It was wrong for us to leave her so far away and alone. I'll never forgive myself."

"I feel the same way, but I doubt if you could have changed anything if you had gone. Do you know what happened?"

"Yes, I think so, but I'm too sad to explain it now. I'll tell you again. We will know so much more about their life there when we read the diary. Oh, poor Aunt Het! I'm glad Rose had some feeling for the child, though, and apparently Abe did too. I think he's watched over her carefully, anyway."

"I'm sure he has. Maybe better in some ways than we could have done. He loves her, too, you know."

The package came several days later. The writing was on old-fashioned bulky foolscap paper. Cecily laid the sheets out on the ironing board and ran a warm iron carefully over the backs to straighten out the folds and wrinkles. They decided at last to read it up in their own room, always together. It was too precious not to be shared.

Rose's Diary

November 12

It's hard for me to go out much now, for I'm so heavy and the doctor thinks I'm safer indoors, for this week the streets are icy. It's been getting colder, and of course I do miss the central heating. I have tried not to let the others know but night before last I couldn't get warm even with the "hot bottle," as Aunt Het calls them, and just kept shivering, so yesterday afternoon Abe said we simply had to move my bed down to the sitting room. I demurred, but he's very obstinate in a nice way, so with Aunt Het's help the bed came down. It's a single one and fits into a sort of corner. It's *such* a comfort to be near the fire. My only real fear was in being so far away from everybody, but Abe solved that at once. He sleeps on the long horsehair sofa in the kitchen and insists it's much better than upstairs for he can study at the kitchen table and then just roll into bed, as it were. I heard him sometime last night very quietly making up the grate fire. It's so very much more comfortable here.

November 20

A strange thing happened a few nights ago. After Abe finishes studying he comes into the sitting room sometimes to talk for a while. There is a small low chair close beside my bed and he sits on that, stretching his long legs out. We had talked about all sorts of things when he suddenly leaned nearer and said he was happy about the baby's coming! Said he could hardly wait. That he had always liked the little young things on the farm, the lambs, and calves and how cunning a brand new colt was. "But," he said, "the baby will be so much more wonderful." I was utterly amazed and I said, "How can you be happy about it when it isn't yours?'' And he said, ''It will be yours, and that is enough for me.'' Then I don't know yet how I ever came to say it. It just seemed to slip out without my thinking, but I said, ''It will be *ours.* '' And in a moment I felt a tear drop on my hand. When I looked up his eyes were swimming. He just said, ''Thank you, Rose,'' and went out of the room.

But since then everything has been different with me. In a way it's a comfort to write it down in this diary for I've kept so much locked up inside me. I would be ashamed to speak of it to anyone. At first when I knew about the baby I hated the very thought of it. And maybe I can't be too much blamed for that. Later on I just felt hard and bitter. And over here when poor Aunt Het talked so much about it I would try to change the subject or even go outdoors to get away from her. She said once she had never known a pregnant woman to be so *modest,* but of course it wasn't that. I just hated to think about it, let alone speak of it.

But after Abe said what he did, it was just as if a black cloud had been lifted from me and everything was light. I began to be happy. I began to realize how wonderful it *would* be to have the baby. For the very first time I wanted it. I keep waking up in the night and thinking about how it will feel in my arms. I found myself singing today, the first since I've been here. Aunt Het was so pleased and surprised. She said she had always liked "a singing woman" though she couldn't raise a tune herself. Abe says we must give her a concert. It's strange how the singing makes me feel more like myself, and therefore happier about the baby, too.

December 1

There has been a queer patch of warmish weather, and the streets are clear of all ice. I have let myself go terribly as far as my hair and my clothes are concerned. I've just been wearing my old sweaters lately. I've been so miserable inside that I didn't care how I looked and hadn't the heart to try to find a Beauty Parlor or a store as Mother told me to. I can't go far, now, but today I discussed it with Aunt Het. It seems that on a funny little street just off this one there are a few shops, so with her arm to lean on (and it's wonderful how strong she is) I went to a small *salon* where under my very definite directions my hair was cut and shaped as it always used to be, and as I looked in the glass I nearly cried. I felt like someone

326

returning from the dead. I sat there to wait while Aunt Het went into a little dress shop beyond, the proprietor of which she knows, and returned with two dresses for me to try. There is nothing like an enceinte condition to win sympathy. I was handled with T.L.C. by all the Beauty ladies and finally in a booth tried on and bought a darling two-piece dress, navy with a white cowl neck. I might as well write it for I would be a fool not to admit it at least to myself. I do *look pretty* in it, and it has certainly raised my spirits.

I rested after we got back and then got all dressed up before Abe came. When he walked into the sitting room and saw me he stood stone still for a minute, and then he did the funniest thing and yet the nicest thing under the circumstances that he could have done for me. *He whistled!*

December 6

We have all been working at the baby's bassinet. It's really just a clothes basket but a nice oval shape and what Aunt Het calls a *willow* basket, much finer than ours back home. Abe has given it three coats of white enamel and you would think it came right out of a store. Abe takes a dim view of my going out again and, besides, a new snow has fallen, so Aunt Het, apparently very proud and delighted to do the errands, has shopped for lining and net, and ribbon which we weave in and out around the top. We have covered one of her softest pillows to put in the bottom and have the little blankets Mother sent folded at the foot. No one would believe how lovely a plain clothes basket could become! Oh, I can never thank Mother enough for hiding the layette in my big bag without telling me. When I finally discovered it I felt almost angry, but now—I take it all out every day along with the other things I have and lay the little garments on the bed and Aunt Het and I pore over them and handle them very gently. They are *so tiny*. I'm beginning to be like Abe. I can hardly wait.

December 14

If I did not feel so happy now about the baby I know I would be homesick with Christmas coming on. I keep picturing all they are doing at home and sometimes I don't hold up too well. However, we are going to do our best to be a little festive. Abe is going to get a little tree and some ornaments. I think I can remember Mother's recipe for the mulled cider and of course I can bake the star cookies. Aunt Het is planning to roast a *goose,* which will be something new to us. She is as excited as a child over everything. Her life really has been lonely. We sang some of "The Student Prince" for her a few nights ago and she sat in her rocking chair perfectly still, just drinking it in, while the tears ran down her cheeks and her hands kept folding and refolding the edge of her white apron. When we finished she said, "Yon was the nicest treat I've had since I was a lassie."

December 20

A very strange thing has happened. I haven't been sleeping well, and when Abe discovered I was lying awake for so long he began coming in with some books to read to me to help pass the hours. I knew he needed his sleep but he insisted. He said it rested his brain after studying so hard on his regular work. Last night he brought in a number of things to read, then at last he put the books down and began to recite a poem he said he was fond of. He said it was called "An Arab Love Song" and he had copied it from one Daddy had given to him when he first began to practice for the play, to help him, he said, from "being so wooden." He has a great

deal of dramatic talent when he lets himself
go and I felt as though I were really there,
under the stars, watching while the young
Arab sang across to his sweetheart in her
family's tent. At the end he looked right into
my eyes as he said the last lines, which I
copied today from his paper.

Leave thy father, leave thy mother
And thy brother;
Leave the black tents of thy tribe apart!
Am I not thy father and thy brother,
And thy mother?
And thou—what needest with thy tribe's
  black tents
Who hast the red pavilion of my heart?

And as he was saying this, looking at me,
I began to blush. I could feel the color
creeping up into my cheeks until I actually
felt hot, and yet I couldn't stop it. Then all
at once he leaned over and kissed me. The
very first time. The tiny peck on the cheek
after the wedding ceremony didn't count, but
this was for *real.* I still couldn't speak, and
we just kept looking at each other. Then he
gathered up his books and papers as though
he were embarrassed and said, "I hope I
haven't offended you, Rose," and went back

to the kitchen. But I lay awake for a long time thinking of it, and I've still been thinking of it today.

December 26

It seems odd to say I have been too busy before this to write in my diary, but that was really true and I'm so thankful it was, for I got over Christmas much better than I had expected. Just one or two quiet little *weeps* when no one knew. We put all the gifts, those from home and our own, under the tree, everything except a little white woolly lamb Abe had found and laid on the bassinet. We had a wonderful dinner and Abe and I did our best with the carols later to please Aunt Het. My mulled cider didn't taste quite like Mother's but wasn't bad and the cookies turned out well. Abe certainly seemed to enjoy them. He has never by word or look acted as though he was thinking of what happened the other night, and I'm so relieved. I have a horror of blushing the way I did then.

The time is really growing quite short now, and I'm glad. The doctor thinks I'll be going to the hospital in one more week at the latest. I have my bag all packed but both Aunt Het and Abe keep saying, "Have you this?'' ''Have you that?'' I tell them they are a pair of fussy old grannies and then we all laugh, which is good for us. The lack of a telephone is awkward, but Aunt Het has arranged with a neighbor who has one so that she can call the doctor any time and Abe too. He has made all sorts of hook-ups at the University about getting a call to him put through fast. Indeed he has thought of everything. I never knew that any *young* man could be as thoughtful and kind as Abe has been to me. Yes and I'll add *tender,* for that has showed so often in his voice, and while for a long time I almost resented it I came to realize that it was helping me more than anything else when I felt so far away and lonely.

January 1

I don't feel well and I guess this is really the day. Aunt Het is out now calling the doctor and Abe. I'll have a lot to write about later on . . .

January 20

I have been back now for a week and can feel my body getting stronger even though my heart is still sore. The first day when Abe told me in the hospital what had happened I couldn't believe it, for all those last weeks it never occurred to me that any harm could come to the baby. I was often a little scared for myself but never for it. I was terribly weak then, and when I heard my hands kept trembling so. Abe took them in his strong ones and sometimes he held them against his cheeks and then somehow I seemed to relax and doze off for a little. I felt such shock that the medicine they gave me didn't have too much effect. Abe stayed all that day till the night nurse came on and by then I was drowsy. I never realized until afterwards that he had had nothing to eat. When the doctor came in to see me the next morning he said I had a wonderful husband, that he had never left me even at the worst and in this case, he added, the staying was not easy.

In spite of everything I gained a little every day. The thing that did hold me back was the awful load of remorse I carried. I finally had to ask the doctor if anything I had done or even *thought* could have caused what happened. He smiled and said, "My dear child, every young mother wonders that, if things go wrong; but I can assure you that this was one of Nature's very, *very* rare mistakes which even we doctors can't explain and that nothing you did or felt or thought had anything whatever to do with it." He was very kind, and I know he felt badly too, for he talked to Abe about it.

January 22

Even now I do get tired when I write much so I'll just make the entries short. Aunt Het says Abe must have carried the little bassinet up to the storeroom in the night for she didn't see him do it. I couldn't shed a tear before, but when she told me this and I thought of the little lamb I cried and cried and I guess it did me good, for I'm not nearly so tense. Also I got out Daddy's letter which he wrote me after Lester Scott was killed, about God not punishing us for our mistakes. Oh, I'm so glad he wrote that to me! That and what the doctor said have eased my mind.

January 24

Abe got the most wonderful report on his work today! We talked about the lines from Shelley that Daddy made us all commit to memory in English: "Many a green isle needs must be . . ." We decided that's the way life is.

It's strange and I really feel so ashamed but it's difficult for me to write home. Abe has been doing that, has given them all details which would have been so hard for me to write, but of course they will be waiting anxiously to hear from me. Yesterday Abe made a suggestion. He knows I've kept a diary since early November and he knows, too, that I get a little nervous and shaky when I think of writing to them just now. He thinks it would please them and be easier for me if I just sent them the diary now and wrote later. At first when I thought of all I've set down here I felt I couldn't do it. But now, I realize there is nothing too intimate for *them* to see. I will add a little more and then let Abe send it off. Of course he doesn't know what is in it. There is so much I would never put in a letter. Maybe it's better this way.

January 26

So this is the end of the Diary. It's a very short one, certainly, but served a purpose when I needed it. I will just close by thanking my father and mother more than my heart can ever express for their brave and incredible kindness to me, and also by telling them a secret. It is that out of this strange and in many ways heart-breaking year for us all there has come to me the most beautiful experience a girl can have. It is still new to me, but I'm sure it will last forever. I am a little shy about writing it down, but surely they should be the first to know.

I have fallen completely, utterly, in love with Abe.

The publishers hope that this Large Print Book has brought you pleasurable reading. Each title is designed to make the text as easy to see as possible. G. K. Hall Large Print Books are available from your library and your local bookstore. Or you can receive information on upcoming and current Large Print Books by mail and order directly from the publisher. Just send your name and address to:

G. K. Hall & Co.
70 Lincoln Street
Boston, Mass. 02111

or call, toll-free:

1-800-343-2806

A note on the text
Large print edition designed by
Bernadette Montalvo.
Composed in 18 pt English Times
on an EditWriter 7700
by Cheryl Ann Yodlin of G.K. Hall Corp.